BARBARIANS

Novels By Robert W. Chambers

Barbarians
The Dark Star
The Girl Philippa
Who Goes There!
Athalie
The Business of Life
The Gay Rebellion
The Streets of Ascalon
The Common Law
The Fighting Chance
The Younger Set
The Danger Mark
The Firing Line
Japonette
Quick Action
The Adventures of
  a Modest Man
Anne's Bridge
Between Friends
The Better Man
Police ! ! !
Some Ladies in Haste
The Tree of Heaven
The Tracer of Lost
  Persons
The Hidden Children

Cardigan
The Reckoning
The Maid-at-Arms
Ailsa Paige
Special Messenger
The Haunts of Men
Lorraine
Maids of Paradise
Ashes of Empire
The Red Republic
Blue-Bird Weather
A Young Man in a
  Hurry
The Green Mouse
Iole
The Mystery of Choice
The Cambric Mask
The Maker of Moons
The King in Yellow
In Search of the
  Unknown
The Conspirators
A King and a Few
  Dukes
In the Quarter
Outsiders

BARBARIANS

BY

ROBERT W. CHAMBERS

WILDSIDE PRESS

TO
LYLE AND MADELEINE MAHAN

I

"Daughter of Light, the bestial wrath
Of Barbary besets thy path!
The Hun is beating his painted drum;
His war horns blare! The Hun is come!"

"Father, I feel his fœtid breath:
The thick air reeks with the stench of death;
My will is Thine. Thy will be done
On Turk and Bulgar, Czech and Hun!"

II

She understands.
Where the dead headland flare
Mocks sea and sand;
Where death-lights shed their glare
On No-Man's-Land.
France takes her stand.
Magnificently fair,
The Flaming Brand
Within her slender hand;
Christ's lilies in her hair.

III

"Daughter of Grief, thy House is sand!
Thy towers are falling athwart the land.
They've flayed the earth to its ribs of chalk
And over its bones the spectres stalk!"

"Father, I see my high spires reel;
My breast is scarred by the Hun's hoofed heel.
What was, shall be! I read Thy sign:
Thy ocean yawns for the smitten swine!"

IV

Then, from Verdun
Pealed westward to the Somme
From every gun
God's summons: "Daughter! Come!"
Then the red sun
Stood still. Grew dumb
The universal hum
Of life, and numb
The lips of Life, undone
By Death. . . . And so—France won!

V

"Daughter of God, the End is here!
The swine rush on: the sea is near!
My wild flowers bloom on the trenches' edge;
My little birds sing by shore and sedge."

"Father, raise up my martyred land!
Clothe her bones with Thy magic hand;
Receive the Brand Thy angel lent,
And stanch my blood with Thy sacrament."

BARBARIANS

CHAPTER I

FED UP

So this is what happened to the dozen-odd malcontents who could no longer stand the dirty business in Europe and the dirtier politicians at home.

There was treachery in the Senate, treason in the House. A plague of liars infested the Republic; the land was rotting with plots.

But if the authorities at Washington remained incredulous, stunned into impotency, while the din of murder filled the world, a few mere men, fed up on the mess, sickened while awaiting executive galvanization, and started east to purge their souls.

They came from the four quarters of the continent, drawn to the decks of the mule transport by a common sickness and a common necessity. Only two among them had ever before met. They represented all sorts, classes, degrees of education and of ignorance, drawn to a common rendezvous by coincidental nausea incident to the temporary stupidity and poltroonery of those supposed to represent them in the Congress of the Great Republic.

The rendezvous was a mule transport reeking with its cargo, still tied up to the sun-scorched wharf where scores of loungers loafed and gazed up at the rail and exchanged badinage with the supercargo.

The supercargo consisted of this dozen-odd fed-up ones—eight Americans, three Frenchmen and one Belgian.

There was a young soldier of fortune named Carfax, recently discharged from the Pennsylvania State Constabulary, who seemed to feel rather sure of a commission in the British service.

Beside him, leaning on the blistering rail, stood a self-possessed young man named Harry Stent. He had been educated abroad; his means were ample; his time his own. He had shot all kinds of big game except a Hun, he told another young fellow—a civil engineer—who

2

stood at his left and whose name was Jim Brown.

A youth on crutches, passing along the deck behind them, lingered, listening to the conversation, slightly amused at Stent's game list and his further ambition to bag a Boche.

The young man's lameness resulted from a trench acquaintance with the game which Stent desired to hunt. His regiment had been, and still was, the 2nd Foreign Legion. He was on his way back, now, to finish his convalescence in his old home in Finistère. He had been a writer of stories for children. His name was Jacques Wayland.

As he turned away from the group at the rail, still amused, a man advancing aft spoke to him by name, and he recognized an American painter whom he had met in Brittany.

"You, Neeland?"

"Oh, yes. I'm fed up with watchful waiting."

"Where are you bound, ultimately?"

"I've a hint that an Overseas unit can use me. And you, Wayland?"

"Going to my old home in Finistère where I'll get well, I hope."

"And then?"

"Second Foreign."

"Oh. Get that leg in the trenches?" inquired Neeland.

"Yes. Came over to recuperate. But Finistère calls me. I've *got* to smell the sea off Eryx before I can get well."

A pleasant-faced, middle-aged man, who stood near, turned his head and cast a professionally appraising glance at the young fellow on crutches.

His name was Vail; he was a physician. It did not seem to him that there was much chance for the lame man's very rapid recovery.

Three muleteers came on deck from below —all young men, all talking in loud, careless voices. They wore uniforms of khaki resembling the regular service uniform. They had no right to these uniforms.

One of these young men had invented the costume. His name was Jack Burley. His two comrades were, respectively, "Sticky"

4

Smith and "Kid" Glenn. Both had figured in the squared circle. All three were fed up. They desired to wallop something, even if it were only a leather-rumped mule.

Four other men completed the supercargo —three French youths who were returning for military duty and one Belgian. They had been waiters in New York. They also were fed up with the administration. They kept by themselves during the voyage. Nobody ever learned their names. They left the transport at Calais, reported, and were lost to sight in the flood of young men flowing toward the trenches.

They completed the odd dozen of fed-up ones who sailed that day on the suffocating mule transport in quest of something they needed but could not find in America—something that lay somewhere amid flaming obscurity in that hell of murder beyond the Somme—their souls' salvation perhaps.

Twelve fed-up men went. And what happened to all except the four French youths is known. Fate laid a guiding hand on the shoulder of Carfax and gave him a gentle shove toward the Vosges. Destiny linked arms with Stent and Brown and led them toward Italy. Wayland's rendezvous with Old Man Death was in Finistère. Neeland sailed with an army corps, but Chance met him at Lorient and led him into the strangest paths a young man ever travelled.

As for Sticky Smith, Kid Glenn and Jack Burley, they were muleteers. Or thought they were. A muleteer has to do with mules. Nothing else is supposed to concern him.

But into the lives of these three muleteers came things never dreamed of in their philosophy—never imagined by them even in their cups.

As for the others, Carfax, Brown, Stent, Wayland, Neeland, this is what happened to each one of them. But the episode of Carfax comes first. It happened somewhere north of the neutral Alpine region where the Vosges shoulder their way between France and Germany.

After he had exchanged a dozen words with a staff officer, he began to realize, vaguely, that he was done in.

CHAPTER II

"Will they do anything for us?" repeated Carfax.

The staff officer thought it very doubtful. He stood in the snow switching his wet puttees and looking out across a world of tumbled mountains. Over on his right lay Germany; on his left, France; Switzerland towered in ice behind him against an arctic blue sky.

It grew warm on the Falcon Peak, almost hot in the sun. Snow was melting on black heaps of rocks; a black salamander, swollen, horrible, stirred from its stiff lethargy and crawled away blindly across the snow.

"Our case is this," continued Carfax; "somebody's made a mistake. We've been forgotten. And if they don't relieve us rather soon

7

some of us will go off our bally nuts. Do you get me, Major?"

"I beg your pardon——"

"Do you understand what I've been saying?"

"Oh, yes; quite so."

"Then ask yourself, Major, how long can four men stand it, cooped up here on this peak? A month, two months, three, five? But it's going on ten months—ten months of solitude—silence—not a sound, except when the snowslides go bellowing off into 'Alsace down there below our feet." His bronzed lip quivered. "I'll get aboard one if this keeps on."

He kicked a lump of ice off into space; the staff officer glanced at him and looked away hurriedly.

"Listen," said Carfax with an effort; "we're not regulars—not like the others. The Canadian division is different. Its discipline is different—in spite of Salisbury Plain and K. of K. In my regiment there are half-breeds, pelt-hunters, Nome miners, Yankees of all degrees, British, Canadians, gentlemen

8

adventurers from Cosmopolis. They're good soldiers, but do you think they'd stay here? It is so in the Athabasca Battalion; it is the same in every battalion. They wouldn't stay here ten months. They couldn't. We are free people; we can't stand indefinite caging; we've got to have walking room once every few months."

The staff officer murmured something.

"I know; but good God, man! Four of us have been on this peak for nearly ten months. We've never seen a Boche, never heard a shot. Seasons come and go, rain falls, snow falls, the winds blow from the Alps, but nothing else comes to us except a half-frozen bird or two."

The staff officer looked about him with an involuntary shiver. There was nothing to see except the sun on the wet, black rocks and the whitewashed observation station of solid stone from which wires sagged into the valley on the French side.

"Well—good luck," he said hastily, looking as embarrassed as he felt. "I'll be toddling along."

"Will you say a word to the General, like a good chap? Tell him how it is with us—four of us all alone up here since the beginning. There's Gary, Captain in the Athabasca Battalion, a Yankee if the truth were known; there's Flint, a cockney lieutenant in a Calgary battery; there's young Gray, a lieutenant and a Prince Edward Islander; and here's me, a major in the Yukon Battalion—four of us on the top of a cursed French mountain—ten months of each other, of solitude, silence—and the whole world rocking with battles—and not a sound up here—not a whisper! I tell you we're four sick men! We've got a grip on ourselves yet, but it's slipping. We're still fairly civil to each other, but the strain is killing. Sullen silences smother irritability, but—" he added in a peculiarly pleasant voice, "I expect we are likely to start killing each other if somebody doesn't get us out of here very damn quick."

The staff captain's lips formed the words, "Awfully sorry! Good luck!" but his articulation was indistinct, and he went off hurriedly, still murmuring.

Carfax stood in the snow, watching him clamber down among the rocks, where an alpinist orderly joined them.

Gary presently appeared at the door of the observation station. "Has he gone?" he inquired, without interest.

"Yes," said Carfax.

"Is he going to do anything for us?"

"I don't know. . . . *No!*"

Gary lingered, kicked at a salamander, then turned and went indoors. Carfax sat down on a rock and sucked at his empty pipe.

Later the three officers in the observation station came out to the door again and looked at him, but turned back into the doorway without saying anything. And after a while Carfax, feeling slightly feverish, went indoors, too.

In the square, whitewashed room Gray and Flint were playing cut-throat poker; Gary was at the telephone, but the messages received or transmitted appeared to be of no importance. There had never been any message of importance from the Falcon Peak or to it. There was likely to be none.

Ennui, inertia, dry rot—and four men, sometimes silently, sometimes violently cursing their isolation, but always cursing it— afraid in their souls lest they fall to cursing one another aloud as they had begun to curse in their hearts.

Months ago rain had fallen; now snow fell, and vast winds roared around them from the Alps. But nothing else ever came to the Falcon Peak, except a fierce, red-eyed *Lämmergeyer* sheering above the peak on enormous pinions, or a few little migrating birds fluttering down, half frozen, from the high air lanes. Now and then, also, came to them a staff officer from below, British sometimes, sometimes French, who lingered no longer than necessary and then went back again, down into friendly deeps where were trees and fields and familiar things and human companionship, leaving them to their hell of silence, of solitude, and of each other.

The tide of war had never washed the base

of their granite cliffs; the highest battle wave
had thundered against the Vosges beyond
earshot; not even a deadened echo of war
penetrated those silent heights; not a Taube
floated in the zenith.

In the squatty, whitewashed ruin which once
had been the eyrie of some petty predatory
despot, and which now served as an observa-
tory for two idle divisions below in the valley, stood three telescopes. Otherwise the
furniture consisted of valises, trunks, a table
and chairs, a few books, several newspapers,
and some tennis balls lying on the floor.

Carfax seated himself at one of the telescopes, not looking through it, his heavy eyes
partly closed, his burnt-out pipe between his
teeth.

Gary rose from the telephone and joined
the card players. They shuffled and dealt
listlessly, seldom speaking save in mono-
syllables.

After a while Carfax went over to the
card table and the young lieutenant cashed in
and took his place at the telescope.

Below in the Alsatian valley spring had

already started the fruit buds, and a delicate green edged the lower snow line.

The lieutenant spoke of it wistfully; nobody paid any attention; he rose presently and went outdoors to the edge of the precipice—not too near, for fear he might be tempted to jump out through the sunshine, down into that inviting world of promise below.

Far underneath him—very far down in the valley—a cuckoo called. Out of the depths floated the elfin halloo, the gaily malicious challenge of spring herself, shouted up melodiously from the plains of Alsace—*Cuckoo! Cuckoo! Cuckoo!*—You poor, sullen, frozen foreigner up there on the snowy rocks!—*Cuckoo! Cuckoo! Cuckoo!*

The lieutenant of Yukon infantry, whose name was Gray, came back into the room.

"There's a bird of sorts yelling like hell below," he said to the card players.

Carfax ran over his cards, rejected three, and nodded. "Well, let him yell," he said.

"What is it, a Boche dicky-bird insulting you?" asked Gary, in his Yankee drawl.

Flint, declining to draw cards, got up and went out into the sunshine. When he returned to the table, he said: "It's a cuckoo. . . . I wish to God I were out of this," he added.

They continued to play for a while without apparent interest. Each man had won his comrades' money too many times to care when Carfax added up debit and credit and wrote down each man's score. In nine months, alternately beggaring one another, they had now, it appeared, broken about even.

Gary, an American in British uniform, twitched a newspaper toward himself, slouched in his chair, and continued to read for a while. The paper was French and two weeks old; he jerked it about irritably.

Gray, resting his elbows on his knees, sat gazing vacantly out of the narrow window. For a smart officer he had grown slovenly.

"If there was any trout fishing to be had," he began; but Flint laughed scornfully.

"What are you laughing at? There must be trout in the valley down there where that bird is," insisted Gray, reddening.

15

"Yes, and there are cows and chickens and houses and women. What of it?"

Gary, in his faded service uniform of a captain, scowled over his newspaper. "It's bad enough to be here," he said heavily; "so don't let's talk about it. Quit disputing."

Flint ignored the order.

"If there was anything sportin' to do——"

"Oh, shut up," muttered Carfax. "Do you expect sport on a hog-back?"

Gray picked up a tennis ball and began to play it against the whitewashed stone wall, using the palm of his hand. Flint joined him presently; Gary went over to the telephone, set the receiver to his ear and spoke to some officer in the distant valley on the French side, continuing a spiritless conversation while watching the handball play. After a while he rose, shambled out and down among the rocks to the spring where snow lay, trodden and filthy, and the big, black salamanders crawled half stupefied in the sun. All his loathing and fear of them kindled again as it always did at sight of them. "Dirty beasts," he muttered, stumping and stumbling among the stunted fir

16

trees; "some day they'll bite some of these damn fools who say they can't bite. And that'll end 'em."

Flint and Gray continued to play handball in a perfunctory way while Carfax looked on from the telephone without interest. Gary came back, his shoes and puttees all over wet snow.

"Unless," he said in a monotonous voice, "something happens within the next few days I'll begin to feel queer in my head; and if I feel it coming on, I'll blow my bally nut off. Or somebody's." And he touched his service automatic in its holster and yawned.

After a dead silence:

"Buck up," remarked Carfax; "think how our men must feel in Belfort, never letting off their guns. Ross rifles, too—not a shot at a Boche since the damn war began!"

"God!" said Flint, smiting the ball with the palm of his hand, "to think of those Ross rifles rusting down there and to think of the pink-skinned pigs they could paunch so cleanly. Did you ever paunch a deer? What a mess of intestines all over the shop!"

17

Gary, still standing, began to kick the snow from his shoes. Gray said to him: "For a dollar of your Yankee money I'd give you a shot at me with your automatic—you're that slack at practice."

"If it goes on much longer like this I'll not have to pay for a shot at anybody," returned Gary, with a short laugh.

Gray laughed too, disagreeably, stretching his facial muscles, but no sound issued.

"We're all going crazy together up here; that's my idea," he said. "I don't know which I can stand most comfortably, your voices or your silence. Both make me sick."

"Some day a salamander will nip you; then you'll go loco," observed Gary, balancing another tennis ball in his right hand. "Give me a shot at you?" he added. "I feel as though I could throw it clean through you. You look soft as a pudding to me."

Far, clear, from infinite depths, the elf-like hail of the cuckoo came floating up to the window.

To Flint, English born, the call meant more than it did to Canadian or Yankee.

18

"In Devon," he said in an altered voice, "they'll be calling just now. There's a world of primroses in Devon. . . . And the thorn is as white as the damned snow is up here."

Gary growled his impatience and his profile of a Greek fighter showed in clean silhouette against the window.

"Aw, hell," he said, "did I come out here for this?—nine months of it?" He hurled the tennis ball at the wall. "Can the home talk, if you don't mind."

The cuckoo was still calling.

"Did you ever play cuckoo," asked Carfax, "at ten shillings a throw? It's not a bad game—if you're put to it for amusement."

Nobody replied; Gray's sunken, boyish face betrayed no interest; he continued to toss a tennis ball against the wall and catch it on the rebound.

Toward sundown the usual Alpine chill set in; a mist hung over the snow-edged cliffs; the rocks breathed steam under a foggy and battered moon.

CHAPTER III

cuckoo!

Carfax, on duty, sat hunched up over the telephone, reporting to the fortress.

Gray came in, closed the wooden shutters, hung blankets over them, lighted an oil stove and then a candle. Flint took up the cards, looked at Gary, then flung them aside, muttering.

Nobody attempted to read; nobody touched the cards again. An orderly came in with soup. The meal was brief and perfectly silent.

Flint said casually, after the table had been cleared: "I haven't slept for a month. If I don't get some sleep I'll go queer. I warn you; that's all. I'm sorry to say it, but it's so."

"They're dirty beasts to keep us here like

this," muttered Gary—"nine months of it, and not a shot."

"There'll be a few shots if things don't change," remarked Flint in a colourless voice. "I'm getting wrong in my head. I can feel it."

Carfax turned from the switchboard with a forced laugh: "Thinking of shooting up the camp?"

"That or myself," replied Flint in a quiet voice; "ever since that cuckoo called I've felt queer."

Gary, brooding in his soiled tunic collar, began to mutter presently: "I once knew a man in a lighthouse down in Florida who couldn't stand it after a bit and jumped off."

"Oh, we've heard that twenty times," interrupted Carfax wearily.

Gray said: "*What* a jump!—I mean down into Alsace below——"

"You're all going dotty!" snapped Carfax. "Shut up or you'll be doing it—some of you."

"I can't sleep. That's where I'm getting queer," insisted Flint. "If I could get a few hours' sleep now——"

"I wish to God the Boches could reach you with a big gun. That would put you to sleep, all right!" said Gray.

"This war is likely to end before any of us see a Fritz," said Carfax. "I could stand it, too, except being up here with such"—his voice dwindled to a mutter, but it sounded to Gary as though he had used the word "rotters."

Flint's face had a white, strained expression; he began to walk about, saying aloud to himself: "If I could only sleep. That's the idea—sleep it off, and wake up somewhere else. It's the silence, or the voices—I don't know which. You dollar-crazy Yankees and ignorant Provincials don't realize what a cuckoo is. You've no traditions, anyway—no past, nothing to care for——"

"Listen to 'Arry!" retorted Gary—"'Arry and his cuckoo!"

Carfax stirred heavily. "Shut up!" he said, with an effort. "The thing is to keep doing something—something—anything — except quarrelling."

He picked up a tennis ball. "Come on, you

funking brutes! I'll teach you how to play cuckoo. Every man takes three tennis balls and stands in a corner of the room. I stand in the middle. Then you blow out the candle. Then I call 'cuckoo!' in the dark and you try to hit me, aiming by the sound of my voice. Every time I'm hit I pay ten shillings to the pool, take my place in a corner, and have a shot at the next man, chosen by lot. And if you throw three balls apiece and nobody hits me, then you each pay ten shillings to me and I'm cuckoo for another round."

"We aim at random?" inquired Gray, mildly interested.

"Certainly. It must be played in pitch darkness. When I call out cuckoo, you take a shot at where you think I am. If you all miss, you all pay. If I'm hit, I pay."

Gary chose three tennis balls and retired to a corner of the room; Gray and Flint, urged into action, took three each, unwillingly.

"Blow out the candle," said Carfax, who had walked into the middle of the room. Gary blew it out and the place was in darkness.

23

They thought they heard Carfax moving cautiously, and presently he called, "Cuckoo!" A storm of tennis balls rebounded from the walls; "Cuckoo!" shouted Carfax, and the tennis balls rained all around him.

Once more he called; not a ball hit him; and he struck a match where he was seated upon the floor.

There was some perfunctory laughter of a feverish sort; the candle was relighted, tennis balls redistributed, and Carfax wrote down his winnings.

The next time, however, Gray, throwing low, caught him. Again the candle was lighted, scores jotted down, a coin tossed, and Flint went in as cuckoo.

It seemed almost impossible to miss a man so near, even in total darkness, but Flint lasted three rounds and was hit, finally, a stinging smack on the ear. And then Gary went in.

It was hot work, but they kept at it feverishly, grimly, as though their very sanity depended upon the violence of their diversion. They threw the balls hard, viciously hard. A sort of silent ferocity seemed to seize them. A chance hit cut the skin over Flint's cheek-bone, and when the candle was lighted, one side of his face was bright with blood.

Early in the proceedings somebody had disinterred brandy and Schnapps from under a bunk. The room had become close; they all were sweating.

Carfax emptied his iced glass, still breathing hard, tossed a shilling and sent in Gary as cuckoo.

Flint, who never could stand spirits, started unsteadily for the candle, but could not seem to blow it out. He stood swaying and balancing on his heels, puffing out his smooth, boyish cheeks and blowing at hazard.

"You're drunk," said Gray, thickly; but he was as flushed as the boy he addressed, only steadier of leg.

"What's that?" retorted Flint, jerking his shoulders around and gazing at Gray out of glassy eyes.

"Blow out that candle," said Gary heavily, "or I'll shoot it out! Do you get that?"

"Shoot!" repeated Flint, staring vaguely

into Gary's bloodshot eyes; "*you* shoot, you old slacker——"

"Shut up and play the game!" cut in Carfax, a menacing roar rising in his voice. "You're all slackers—and rotters, too. Play the game! Keep playing—hard!—or you'll go clean off your fool nuts!"

Gary walked heavily over and knocked the tennis balls out of Flint's hands.

"There's a better game than that," he said, his articulation very thick; "but it takes nerve—if you've got it, you spindle-legged little cockney!"

Flint struck at him aimlessly. "I've got nerve," he muttered, "plenty of nerve, old top! What d'you want? I'm your man; I'll go you—eh, what?"

"Go on with the game, I tell you!" bawled Carfax.

Gary swung around: "Wait till I explain——"

"No, don't wait! Keep going! Keep playing! Keep doing something, for God's sake!"

"Will you wait!" shouted Gary. "I want to tell you——"

Carfax made a hopeless gesture: "It's talk that will do the trick for us all——"

"I want to tell you——"

Carfax shrugged, emptied his full glass with a gesture of finality.

"Then talk, damn you! And we'll all be at each other's throats before morning."

Gary got Gray by the elbow: "Reggie, it's this way. We flip up for cuckoo. Whoever gets stuck takes a shot apiece from our automatics in the legs—eh, what?"

"It's perfectly agreeable to me," assented Gray, in the mincing, elaborate voice characteristic of him when drunk.

Flint wagged his head. "It's a sportin' game. I'm in," he said.

Gary looked at Carfax. "A shot in the dark at a man's legs. And if he gets his— it will be Blighty in exchange for hell."

Carfax, sullen with liquor, shoved his big hand into his pocket, produced a shilling, and tossed it.

A brighter flush stained the faces which

ringed him; the risky hazard of the affair cleared their sick minds to comprehension.

Tails turned uppermost; Flint and Gary were eliminated. It lay between Carfax and Gray, and the older man won.

"Mind you fire low," said the young fellow, with an excited laugh, and walked into the middle of the room.

Gary blew out the candle. Presently from somewhere in the intense darkness Gray called "Cuckoo!" and instantly a slanting red flash lashed out through the gloom. And, when the deafening echo had nearly ceased: "Cuckoo!"

Another pistol crashed. And after a swimming interval they heard him moving. "Cuckoo!" he called; a level flame stabbed the dark; something fell, thudding through the staccato uproar of the explosion. At the same moment the outer door opened on the crack and Carfax's orderly peeped in.

Carfax struck a match with shaky fingers; the candle guttered, sank, flared on Flint, who was laughing without a sound. "Got the beggar, by God!" he whispered—

"through the head! Look at him. Look at Reggie Gray! Tried for his head and got him——"

He reeled back, chuckling foolishly, and levelled at Carfax. "Now I'll get you!" he simpered, and shot him through the face.

As Carfax pitched forward, Gary fired.

"Missed me, by God!" laughed Flint. "Shoot? Hell, yes. I'll show you how to shoot——"

He struck the lighted candle with his left hand and laughed again in the thick darkness.

"Shoot? I'll show you how to shoot, you old slacker——"

Gary fired.

After a silence Flint giggled in the choking darkness as the door opened cautiously again, and shot at the terrified orderly.

"I'm a cockney, am I? And you don't think much of the Devon cuckoos, do you? Now I'll show you that I understand all kinds of cuckoos——"

Both flashes split the obscurity at the same moment. Flint fell back against the wall and slid down to the floor. The outer door began to open again cautiously.

But the orderly, half dressed, remained knee-deep in the snow by the doorway.

After a long interval Gary struck a match, then went over and lit the candle. And, as he turned, Flint fired from where he lay on the floor and Gary swung heavily on one heel, took two uncertain steps. Then his pistol fell clattering; he sank to his knees and collapsed face downward on the stones.

Flint, still lying where he had fallen, partly upright, against the wall, began to laugh, and died a few moments later, the wind from the slowly opening door stirring his fair hair and extinguishing the candle.

And at last, through the opened door crept Carfax's orderly; peered into the darkness within, shivering in his unbuttoned tunic, his boots wet with snow.

Dawn already whitened the east; and up out of the ghastly fog edging the German Empire, silhouetted, monstrous, against the daybreak, soared a *Lämmergeyer,* beating the livid void with enormous, unclean wings.

The orderly heard its scream, shrank, cowering, against the door frame as the huge bird's ferocious red and yellow eyes blazed level with his.

Suddenly, above the clamor of the *Lämmergeyer,* the shrill bell of the telephone began to ring.

The terrible racket of the *Lämmergeyer* filled the sky; the orderly stumbled into the room, slipped in a puddle of something wet, sent an empty bottle rolling and clinking away into the darkness; stumbled twice over prostrate bodies; reached the telephone, half fainting; whispered for help.

After a long, long while, the horror still thickly clogging vein and brain, he scratched a match, hesitated, then holding it high, reeled toward the door with face averted.

Outside the sun was already above the horizon, flashing over Haut Alsace at his feet.

The *Lämmergeyer* was a speck in the sky, poised over France.

Up out of the infinite and sunlit chasm came a mocking, joyous hail—up through the sheer, misty gulf out of vernal depths: *Cuck*-oo! *Cuck*-oo! *Cuck*-oo!

CHAPTER IV

RECONNAISSANCE

And that was the way Carfax ended—a tiny tragedy of incompetence compared to the mountainous official fiasco at Gallipoli. Here, a few perished among the filthy salamanders in the snow; there, thousands died in the burning Turkish gorse——

But that's history; and its makers are already officially damned.

But now concerning two others of the fed-up dozen on board the mule transport—Harry Stent and Jim Brown. Destiny linked arms with them; Fate jerked a mysterious thumb over her shoulder toward Italy. Chance detailed them for special duty as soon as they landed.

It was a magnificent sight, the disembarking of the British overseas military force sent secretly into Italy.

They continued to disembark and entrain at night. Nobody knew that British troops were in Italy.

The infernal uproar along the Isonzo never ceased; the din of the guns resounded through the Trentino, but British and Canadian noses were sniffing at something beyond the Carnic Alps, along the slopes of which they continued to concentrate, Rifles, Kilties, and Gunners.

There seemed to be no particular hurry. Details from the Canadian contingent were constantly sent out to familiarize themselves with the vast waste of tunneled mountains denting the Austrian sky-line to the northward; and all day long Dominion reconnoitering parties wandered among valleys, alms, forest, and peaks in company sometimes with Italian alpinists, sometimes by themselves, prying, poking, snooping about with all the emotionless pertinacity of Teuton tourists preoccupied with *wanderlust, kultur,* and *ewigkeit.*

And one lovely September morning the British Military Observer with the Italian army, and his very British aid, sat on a sunny rock on the Col de la Reine and watched a Canadian northward reconnaissance—nothing much to see, except a solitary moving figure here and there on the mountains, crawling like a deerstalker across ledges and stretches of bracken—a few dots on the higher slopes, visible for a moment, then again invisible, then glimpsed against some lower snow patch, and gone again beyond the range of powerful glasses.

"The Athabasca regiment, 13th Battalion," remarked the British Military Observer; "lively and rather noisy."

"Really," observed his A. D. C.

"Sturdy, half-disciplined beggars," continued the B. M. O., watching the mountain plank through his glasses; "every variety of adventurer in their ranks—cattlemen, ranchmen, Hudson Bay trappers, North West police, lumbermen, mail carriers, bear hunters, Indians, renegade frontiersmen, soldiers of fortune—a sweet lot, Algy."

"Ow."

"—And half of 'em unruly Yankees—the most objectionable half, you know."

"A bad lot," remarked the Honorable Algy.

"Not at all," said the B. M. O. complacently; "I've a relative of sorts with 'em—leftenant, I believe—a Yankee brother-in-law, in point of fact."

"Ow."

"Married a step-sister in the States. Must look him up some day," concluded the B. M. O., adjusting his field glasses and focussing them on two dark dots moving across a distant waste of alpine roses along the edge of a chasm.

One of the dots happened to be the "relative of sorts" just mentioned; but the B. M. O. could not know that. And a moment afterward the dots became invisible against the vast mass of the mountain, and did not again reappear within the field of the English officer's limited vision. So he never knew he had seen his relative of sorts.

Up there on the alp, one of the dots, which at near view appeared to be a good-looking, bronzed young man in khaki, puttees, and mountain shoes, said to the other officer who was scrambling over the rocks beside him:

"Did you ever see a better country for sheep?"

"Bear, elk, goats—it's sure a great layout," returned the younger officer, a Canadian whose name was Stent.

"Goats," nodded Brown—"sheep and goats. This country was made for them. I fancy they *have* chamois here. Did you ever see one, Harry?"

"Yes. They have a thing out here, too, called an ibex. You never saw an ibex, did you, Jim?"

Brown, who had halted, shook his head. Stent stepped forward and stood silently beside him, looking out across the vast cleft in the mountains, but not using his field glasses.

At their feet the cliffs fell away sheer into tremendous and dizzying depths; fir forests far below carpeted the abyss like wastes of velvet moss, amid which glistened a twisted silvery thread—a river. A world of mountains bounded the horizon.

"Better make a note or two," said Stent briefly.

They unslung their rifles, seated themselves in the warm sun amid a deep thicket of alpine roses, and remained silent and busy with pencil and paper for a while—two inconspicuous, brownish-grey figures, cuddled close among the greyish rocks, with nothing of military insignia about their dress or their round grey wool caps to differentiate them from sportsmen—wary stalkers of chamois or red deer—except that under their unbelted tunics automatics and cartridge belts made perceptible bunches.

Just above them a line of stunted firs edged limits of perpetual snow, and rocks and glistening fields of crag-broken white carried the eye on upward to the dazzling pinnacle of the Col de la Reine, splitting the vast, calm blue above.

Nothing except peaks disturbed the tranquil sky to the northward; not a cloud hung there. But westward mist clung to a few mountain flanks, and to the east it was snowing on distant crests.

Brown, sketching rapidly but accurately, laughed a little under his breath.

"To think," he said, "not a Boche dreams we are in the Carnic Alps. It's very funny, isn't it? Our surveyors are likely to be here in a day or two, I fancy."

Stent, working more slowly and methodically on his squared map paper, the smoke drifting fragrantly from his brier pipe, nodded in silence, glancing down now and then at the barometer and compass between them.

"Mentioning big game," he remarked presently, "I started to tell you about the ibex, Jim. I've hunted a little in the Eastern Alps."

"I didn't know it," said Brown, interested.

"Yes. A classmate of mine at the Munich Polytechnic invited me—Siurd von Glahn—a splendid fellow—educated at Oxford—just like one of us—nothing of the Boche about him at all——"

Brown laughed: "A Boche is always a Boche, Harry. The black Prussian blood——"

"No; Siurd was all white. Really. A charming, lovable fellow. Anyway, his dad had a shooting where there were chamois, reh, hirsch, and the king of all Alpine big game—ibex. And Siurd asked me."

"Did you get an ibex?" inquired Brown, sharpening his pencil and glancing out across the valley at a cloud which had suddenly formed there.

"I did."

"What manner of beast is it?"

"It has mountain sheep and goats stung to death. Take it from me, Jim, it's the last word in mountain sport. The chamois isn't in it. Pooh, I've seen chamois within a hundred yards of a mountain macadam highway. But the ibex? Not much! The man who stalks and kills an ibex has nothing more to learn about stalking. Chamois, red deer, Scotch stag make you laugh after you've done your bit in the ibex line."

"How about our sheep and goat?" inquired Brown, staring at his comrade.

"It's harder to get ibex."

"Nonsense!"

"It really is, Jim."

"What does your ibex resemble?"

"It's a handsome beast, ashy grey in summer, furred a brownish yellow in winter, and with little chin whiskers and a pair of big, curved, heavily ridged horns, thick and flat and looking as though they ought to belong to something African, and twice as big."

"Some trophy, what?" commented Brown, working away at his sketches.

"Rather. The devilish thing lives along the perpetual snow line; and, for incredible stunts in jumping and climbing, it can give points to any Rocky Mountain goat. You try to get above it, spend the night there, and stalk it when it returns from nocturnal grazing in the stunted growth below. That's how."

"And you got one?"

"Yes. It took six days. We followed it for that length of time across the icy mountains, Siurd and I. I thought I'd die."

"Cold work, eh?"

Stent nodded, pocketed his sketch, fished out a packet of bread and chocolate from his pocket and, rolling over luxuriously in the sun among the alpine roses, lunched leisurely, flat on his back.

Brown presently stretched out and reclined on his elbow; and while he ate he lazily watched a kestrel circling deep in the gulf below him.

"I think," he said, half to himself, "that this is the most beautiful region on earth."

Stent lifted himself on both elbows and gazed across the chasm at the lower slopes of the alm opposite, all ablaze with dewy wild flowers. Down it, between fern and crag and bracken, flashed a brook, broken into in silvery sections amid depths of velvet green below, where evidently it tumbled headlong into that thin, shining thread which was a broad river.

"Yes," mused Stent, "Siurd von Glahn and I were comrades on many a foot tour through such mountains as these. He was a delightful fellow, my classmate Siurd——"

Brown's swift rigid grip on his arm checked him to silence; there came the clink of an iron-shod foot on the ledge; they snatched their rifles from the fern patch; two figures stepped around the shelf of rock, looming up dark against the dazzling sky.

CHAPTER V.

Brown, squatting cross-legged among the alpine roses, squinted along his level rifle.

"Halt!" he said with a pleasant, rising inflection in his quiet voice. "Stand very still, gentlemen," he added in German.

"Drop your rifles. Drop 'em quick!" he repeated more sharply. "Up with your hands —hold them up high! Higher, if you please!— quickly. Now, then, what are you doing on this alp?"

What they were doing seemed apparent enough—two gentlemen of Teutonic persuasion, out stalking game—deer, rehbok or chamois—one a tall, dark, nice-looking young fellow wearing the usual rough gray jacket with stag-horn buttons, green felt hat with feather, and leather breeches of the alpine hunter. His

43

knees and aristocratic ankles were bare and bronzed. He laughed a little as he held up his arms.

The other man was stout and stocky rather than fat. He had the square red face and bushy beard of a beer-nourished Teuton and the spectacles of a Herr Professor. He held up his blunt hands with all ten stubby fingers spread out wide. They seemed rather soiled.

From his *rücksack* stuck out a butterfly net in two sections and the deeply scalloped, silver-trimmed butt of a sporting rifle. Edelweiss adorned his green felt hat; a green tin box punched full of holes was slung from his broad shoulders.

Brown, lowering his rifle cautiously, was already getting to his feet from the trampled bracken, when, behind him, he heard Stent's astonished voice break forth in pedantic German:

"Siurd! Is it *thou* then?"

"Harry Stent!" returned the dark, nice-looking young fellow amiably. And, in a delightful voice and charming English:

"Pray, am I to offer you a shake hands," he

inquired smilingly; "or shall I continue to in-
voke the Olympian gods with classically uplifted and imploring arms?"

Brown let Stent pass forward. Then, stepping back, he watched the greeting between
these two old classmates. His rifle, grasped
between stock and barrel, hung loosely between
both hands. His expression became vacantly
good humoured; but his brain was working like
lightning.

Stent's firm hand encountered Von Glahn's
and held it in questioning astonishment. Looking him in the eyes he said slowly: "Siurd, it
is good to see you again. It is amazing to
meet you this way. I am glad. I have never
forgotten you. . . . Only a moment ago I was
speaking to Brown about you—of our wonderful ibex hunt! I was telling Brown—my
comrade—" he turned his head slightly and
presented the two young men—"Mr. Brown,
an American——"

"American?" repeated Von Glahn in his gentle, well-bred voice, offering his hand. And, in
turn, becoming sponsor, he presented his stocky
companion as Dr. von Dresslin; and the cere-

mony instantly stiffened to a more rigid etiquette.

Then, in his always gentle, graceful way, Von Glahn rested his hand lightly on Stent's shoulder:

"You made us jump—you two Americans—as though you had been British. Of what could two Americans be afraid in the Carnic Alps to challenge a pair of wandering ibex stalkers?"

"You forget that I am Canadian," replied Stent, forcing a laugh.

"At that, you are practically American and civilian—" He glanced smilingly over their equipment, carelessly it seemed to Stent, as though verifying all absence of military insignia. "Besides," he added with his gentle humour, "there are no British in Italy. And no Italians in these mountains, I fancy; they have their own affairs to occupy them on the Isonzo I understand. Also, there is no war between Italy and Germany."

Stent smiled, perfectly conscious of Brown's telepathic support in whatever was now to pass between them and these two Germans. He knew, and Brown knew, that these Germans must be taken back as prisoners; that, suspicious or not, they could not be permitted to depart again with a story of having met an American and a Canadian after ibex among the Carnic Alps.

These two Germans were already their prisoners; but there was no hurry about telling them so.

"How do you happen to be here, Siurd?" asked Stent, frankly curious.

Von Glahn lifted his delicately formed eyebrows, then, amused:

"Count von Plessis invites me; and"—he laughed outright—"he must have invited you, Harry, unless you are poaching!"

"Good Lord!" exclaimed Stent, for a brief second believing in the part he was playing; "I supposed this to be a free alp."

He and Von Glahn laughed; and the latter said, still frankly amused: *"Soyez tranquille,* Messieurs; Count von Plessis permits my friends—in my company—to shoot the Queen's alm."

With a lithe movement, wholly graceful, he

slipped the *rücksack* from his shoulders, let it fall among the *alpenrosen* beside his sporting rifle.

"We have a long day and a longer night ahead of us," he said pleasantly, looking from Stent to Brown. "The snow limit lies just above us; the ibex should pass here at dawn on their way back to the peak. Shall we consolidate our front, gentlemen—and make it a Quadruple Entente?"

Stent replied instantly: "We join you with thanks, Siurd. My one ibex hunt is no experience at all compared to your record of a veteran—" He looked full and significantly at Brown; continuing: "As you say, we have all day and—a long night before us. Let us make ourselves comfortable here in the sun before we take—our final stations."

And they seated themselves in the lee of the crag, foregathering fraternally in the warm alpine sunshine.

The Herr Professor von Dresslin grunted as he sat down. After he had lighted his pipe he grunted again, screwed together his butterfly net and gazed hard through thick-lensed spectacles at Brown.

"Does it interest you, sir, the pursuit of the diurnal Lepidoptera?" he inquired, still staring intently at the American.

"I don't know anything about them," explained Brown. "What are Lepidoptera?"

"The *schmetterling*—the butterfly. In Amerika, sir, you have many fine species, notably Parnassus clodius and the Parnassus smintheus of the four varietal forms." His prominent eyes shifted from one detail of Brown's costume to another—not apparently an intelligent examination, but a sort of protruding and indifferent stare.

His gaze, however, was arrested for a moment where the lump under Brown's tunic indicated something concealed—a hunting knife, for example. Brown's automatic was strapped there. But the bulging eyes, expressionless still, remained fixed for a second only, then travelled on toward the Ross rifle—the Athabasca Regiment having been permitted to exchange this beloved weapon for the British regulation piece recently issued to the Canadians. From behind the thick lenses of his spectacles the Herr Professor examined the rifle while his monotonously dreary voice continued an entomological monologue for Brown's edification. And all the while Von Glahn and Stent, reclining nearby among the ferns, were exchanging what appeared to be the frankest of confidences and the happiest of youthful reminiscences.

"Of the Parnassians," rumbled on Professor von Dresslin, "here in the Alps we possess one notable example—namely, the Parnassus Apollo. It is for the capture of this never-to-be-sufficiently studied butterfly that I have, upon this ibex-hunting expedition, myself equipped with net and suitable paraphernalia."

"I see," nodded Brown, eyeing the green tin box and the net. The Herr Professor's pop-eyed attention was now occupied with the service puttees worn by Brown. A sportsman also might have worn them, of course.

"The Apollo butterfly," droned on Professor Dresslin, "iss a butterfly of the larger magnitude among European Lepidoptera, yet not of the largest. The Parnassians, allied to the

Papilionidæ, all live only in high altitudes, and are, by the thinly scaled and always-to-be-remembered red and plack ge-spotted wings, to be readily recognized. I haf already two specimens captured this morning. I haff the honour, sir, to exhibit them for your inspection——"

He fished out a flat green box from his pocket, opened it under Brown's nose, leaning close enough to touch Brown with an exploring and furtive elbow—and felt the contour of the automatic.

Amid a smell of carbolic and camphor cones Brown beheld, pinned side by side upon the cork-lined interior of the box, two curiously pretty butterflies.

Their drooping and still pliable wings seemed as thin as white tissue paper; their bodies were covered with furry hairs. Brick-red and black spots decorated the frail membrane of the wings in a curiously pleasing harmony of pattern and of colour.

"Very unusual," he said, with a vague idea he was saying the wrong thing.

Monotonously, paying no attention, Professor

von Dresslin continued: "I, the life history of the Parnassus Apollo, haff from my early youth investigated with minuteness, diligence, and patience."—His protuberant eyes were now fixed on Brown's rifle again.—"For many years I haff bred this Apollo butterfly from the egg, from the caterpillar, from the chrysalis. I have the negroid forms, the albino forms, the dwarf forms, the hybrid forms investigated under effery climatic condition. Notes sufficient for three volumes of quarto already exist as a residuum of my investigations——"

He looked up suddenly into the American's face—which was the first sudden movement the Herr Professor had made——

"Ach wass! Three volumes! It is nothing. There iss material for thirty!—A lifetime iss too short to know all the secrets of a single species. . . . If I may inquire, sir, of what pattern is your most interesting and admirable rifle?"

"A—Ross," said Brown, startled into a second's hesitation.

"So? And, if I may inquire, of what nationality iss it, a R-r-ross?"

"It's a Canadian weapon. We Americans use it a great deal for big game."

"So? . . . And it iss also by the Canadian military employed perhaps, sir?"

"I believe," said Brown, carelessly, "that the British Government has taken away the Ross rifle from the Canadians and given them the regulation weapon."

"So? Permit—that I examine, sir?"

Brown did not seem to hear him or notice the extended hand—blunt-fingered, hairy, persistent.

The Professor, not discouraged, repeated: "Sir, *bitte darf ich*, may I be permitted?" And Brown's eyes flashed back a lightning shaft of inquiry. Then, carelessly smiling, he passed the Ross rifle over to the Herr Professor; and, at the same time, drew toward him that gentleman's silver-mounted weapon, and carelessly cocked it.

"Permit me," he murmured, balancing it innocently in the hollow of his left arm, apparently preoccupied with admiration at the florid workmanship of stock and guard. No movement that the Herr Professor made escaped

him; but presently he thought to himself—
"The old dodo is absolutely unsuspicious. My
nerves are out of order. . . . What odd eyes
that Fritz has!"

When Herr Professor von Dresslin passed
back the weapon Brown laid the German sporting piece beside it with murmured complimen-
tary comment.

"Yess," said the German, "such rifles kill
when properly handled. We Germans may
cordially recommend them for our Américan
—friends—" Here was the slightest hesitation—"Pardon! I mean that we may safely
guarantee this rifle *to* our friends."

Brown looked thoughtfully at the thick lenses
of the spectacles. The popeyes remained expressionless, utterly, Teutonically inscrutable.
A big heather bee came buzzing among the
alpenrosen. Its droning hum resembled the
monotone of the Herr Professor.

Behind them Brown heard Stent saying: "Do
you remember our ambition to wear the laurels
of Parnassus, Siurd? Do you remember our
notes at the lectures on the poets? And our

54

ambition to write at least one deathless poem apiece before we died?"

Von Glahn's dark eyes narrowed with merriment and his gentle laugh and attractive voice sounded pleasantly in Brown's ears.

"You wrote at least *one* famous poem to Rosa," he said, still laughing.

"To Rosa? Oh! Rosa of the Café Luitpold! By Jove I did, didn't I, Siurd? How on earth did you ever remember that?"

"I thought it very pretty." He began to repeat aloud:

> "Rosa with the winsome eyes,
> When my beer you bring to me;
> I can see through your disguise!
> I my goddess recognize—
> Hebe, young immortally,
> Sweet nepenthe pouring me!"

Stent laughed outright:

"How funny to think of it now—and to think of Rosa! . . . And you, Siurd, do you forget that you also composed a most wonderful war-poem—to the metre of 'Fly, Eagle, Fly!' Do you remember how it began?

"Slay, Eagle, Slay!
  They die who dare decry us!
Red dawns 'The Day.'
  The western cliffs defy us!
Turn their grey flood
To seas of blood!
And, as they flee, Slay, Eagle! Slay!
For God has willed this German 'Day'!"

"Enough," said Siurd Von Glahn, still laughing, but turning very red. "What a terrible memory you have, Harry! For heaven's sake spare my modesty such accurate reminiscences."

"I thought it fine poetry—then," insisted Stent with a forced smile. But his voice had subtly altered.

They looked at each other in silence, the reminiscent smile still stamped upon their stiffening lips.

For a brief moment the years had seemed to fade—time was not—the sunshine of that careless golden age had seemed to warm them once again there where they sat amid the *alpenrosen* below the snow line on the Col de la Reine.

But it did not endure; everything concerning earth and heaven and life and death had so far remained unsaid between these two. And never would be said. Both understood that, perhaps.

Then Von Glahn's sidelong and preoccupied glance fell on Stent's field glasses slung short around his neck. His rigid smile died out. Soldiers wore field glasses that way; hunters, when they carried them instead of spyglasses, wore them *en bandoulière*.

He spoke, however, of other matters in his gentle, thoughtful voice—avoiding always any mention of politics and war—chatted on pleasantly with the familiarity and insouciance of old acquaintance. Once he turned slowly and looked at Brown—addressed him politely—while his dark eyes wandered over the American, noting every detail of dress and equipment, and the slight bulge at his belt line beneath the tunic.

Twice he found pretext to pick up his rifle, but discarded it carelessly, apparently not noticing that Stent and Brown always resumed their own weapons when he touched his.

Brown said to Von Glahn:

"Ibex stalking is a new game to me. My friend Stent tells me that you are old at it."

"I have followed some few ibex, Mr. Brown," replied the young man modestly. "And—other game," he added with a shrug.

"I know how it's done in theory," continued the American; "and I am wondering whether we are to lie in this spot until dawn tomorrow or whether we climb higher and lie in the snow up there"

"In the snow, perhaps. God knows exactly where we shall lie tonight—Mr. Brown."

There was an odd look in Siurd's soft brown eyes; he turned and spoke to Herr Professor von Dresslin, using dialect—and instantly appearing to recollect himself he asked pardon of Stent and Brown in his very perfect English.

"I said to the Herr Professor in the Traun dialect: 'Ibex may be stirring, as it is already late afternoon. We ought now to use our glasses.' My family," he added apologetically, "come from the Traunwald; I forget and employ the vernacular at times."

The Herr Professor unslung his telescope, set his rifle upright on the moss, and, kneeling, balanced the long spyglass alongside of the blued-steel barrel, resting it on his hand as an archer fits the arrow he is drawing on the bowstring.

Instantly both Brown and Stent thought of the same thing: the chance that these Germans might spy others of the Athabasca regiment prowling among the ferns and rocks of neighbouring slopes. The game was nearly at an end, anyway.

They exchanged a glance; both picked up their rifles; Brown nodded almost imperceptibly. The tragic comedy was approaching its close.

"*Hirsch*," grunted the Herr Professor—"*und stück*—on the north alm"—staring through his telescope intently.

"Accorded," said Siurd Von Glahn, balancing his spyglass and sweeping the distant crags. "*Stück* on the western shoulder," he added— "and a stag royal among them."

"Of ten?"

"Of twelve."

After a silence: "Why are they galloping—
I wonder—the herd-stag and *stück?*"

Brown very quietly laid one hand on Stent's
arm.

"A *geier,* perhaps," suggested Siurd, his eye
glued to his spyglass.

"No ibex?" asked Stent in a voice a little
forced.

"Noch nicht, mon ami. Tiens! A *gemsbok*—
high on the third peak—feeding."

"Accorded," grunted the Herr Professor
after an interval of search; and he closed his
spyglass and placed his rifle on the moss.

His staring, protuberant eyes fell casually
upon Brown, who was laying aside his own
rifle again—and the German's expression did
not alter.

"Ibex!" exclaimed Von Glahn softly.

Stent, rising impulsively to his feet, brack-
etted his field glasses on the third peak, and
stood there, poised, slim and upright against
the sky on the chasm's mossy edge.

"I don't see your ibex, Siurd," he said, still
searching.

"On the third peak, *mon ami"*—drawing

Stent familiarly to his side—the lightest caressing contact—merely enough to verify the existence of the automatic under his old classmate's tunic.

If Stent did not notice the impalpable touch, neither did Brown notice it, watching them. Perhaps the Herr Professor did, but it is not at all certain, because at that moment there came flopping along over the bracken and *alpenrosen* a loppy winged butterfly—a large, whitish creature, seeming uncertain in its irresolute flight whether to alight at Brown's feet or go flapping aimlessly on over Brown's head.

The Herr Professor snatched up his net—struck heavily toward the winged thing—a silent, terrible, sweeping blow with net and rifle clutched together. Brown went down with a crash.

At the shocking sound of the impact Stent wheeled from the abyss, then staggered back under the powerful shove from Von Glahn's nervous arm. Swaying, fighting frantically for foothold, there on the chasm's awful edge, he balanced for an instant; fought for equilibrium. Von Glahn, rigid, watched him. Then, deathly white, his young eyes looking straight into the eyes of his old classmate—Stent lost the fight, fell outward, wider, dropping back into mid-air, down through sheer, tremendous depths—down there where the broad river seemed only a silver thread and the forests looked like beds of tender, velvet moss.

After him, fluttering irresolutely, flitted Parnassus Apollo, still winging its erratic way where God willed it—a frail, dainty, translucent, wind-blown fleck of white above the gulf —symbol, perhaps of the soul already soaring up out of the terrific deeps below.

The Herr Professor sweated and panted as he tugged at the silk handkerchief with which he was busily knotting the arms of the unconscious American behind his back.

"Pouf! Ugh! Pig-dog!" he grunted—"mit his pockets full of automatic clips. A Yankee, eh? What I tell you, Siurd?—English and Yankee they are one in blood and one at heart—pig-dogs effery one. Hey, Siurd, what I told you already *gesternabend?* The British *schwein* are in Italy already. Hola! Siurd! Take his feet and we turn him over *mal!*"

But Von Glahn remained motionless, leaning heavily against the crag, his back to the abyss, his blond head buried in both arms.

So the Herr Professor, who was a major, too, began, with his powerful, stubby hands, to pull the unconscious man over on his back. And, as he worked, he hummed monotonously but contentedly in his bushy beard something about *something* being *"über alles"*—God, perhaps, perhaps the blue sky overhead which covered him and his sickened friend alike, and the hurt enemy whose closed lids shut out the sky above —and the dead man lying very, very far below them—where river and forest and moss and Parnassus were now alike to him.

CHAPTER VI

IN FINISTÈRE

It was a dirty trick that they played Stent and Brown—the three Mysterious Sisters, Fate, Chance, and Destiny. But they're always billed for any performance, be it vaudeville or tragedy; and there's no use hissing them off: they'll dog you from the stage entrance if they take a fancy to you.

They dogged Wayland from the dock at Calais, where the mule transport landed, all the way to Paris, then on a slow train to Quimperlé, and then, by stagecoach, to that little lost house on the moors, where ties held him most closely—where all he cared for in this world was gathered under a humble roof.

In spite of his lameness he went duck-shooting the week after his arrival. It was rather forcing his convalescence, but he believed it would accelerate it to go about in the open air, as though there were nothing the matter with his shattered leg.

So he hobbled down to the point he knew so well. He had longed for the sea off Eryx. It thundered at his feet.

And, now, all around him through clamorous obscurity a watery light glimmered; it edged the low-driven clouds hurrying in from the sea; it outlined the long point of rocks thrust southward into the smoking smother.

The din of the surf filled his ears; through flying patches of mist he caught glimpses of rollers bursting white against the reef; heard duller detonations along unseen sands, and shattering reports where heavy waves exploded among basalt rocks.

His lean face of an invalid glistened with spray; salt water dripped from cap and coat, spangled the brown barrels of his fowling-piece, and ran down the varnished supports of both crutches where he leaned on them, braced forward against an ever-rising wind.

At moments he seemed to catch glimpses of darker specks dotting the heaving flank of some huge wave. But it was not until the wild ducks rose through the phantom light and came whirring in from the sea that his gun, poked stiffly skyward, flashed in the pallid void. And then, sometimes, he hobbled back after the dead quarry while it still drove headlong inland, slanting earthward before the gale.

Once, amid the endless thundering, in the turbulent desolation around him, through the roar of wind in his ears, he seemed to catch deadened sounds resembling distant seaward cannonading — *real* cannonading — as though individual shots, dully distinct, dominated for a few moments the unbroken uproar of surf and gale.

He listened, straining his ears, alert, intent upon the sounds he ought to recognize —the sounds he knew so well.

Only the ceaseless pounding of the sea assailed his ears.

Three wild duck, widgeon, came speeding through the fog; he breasted the wind, balanced heavily on both crutches and one leg, and shoved his gun upward.

At the same instant the mist in front and

overhead became noisy with wild fowl, rising in one great, panic-stricken, clamoring cloud. He hesitated; a muffled, thudding sound came to him over the unseen sea, growing louder, nearer, dominating the gale, increasing to a rattling clatter.

Suddenly a great cloudy shape loomed up through the whirling mist ahead—an enormous shadow in the fog—a gigantic spectre rushing inland on vast and ghostly pinions.

As the man shrank on his crutches, looking up, the aëroplane swept past overhead— a wounded, wavering, unsteady, unbalanced thing, its right aileron dangling, half stripped, and almost mangled to a skeleton.

Already it was slanting lower toward the forest like a hard-hit duck, wing-crippled, fighting desperately for flight-power to the very end. Then the inland mist engulfed it.

And after it hobbled Wayland, painfully, two brace of dead ducks and his slung fowling piece bobbing on his back, his rubber-shod crutches groping and probing among drenched rocks and gullies full of kelp, his left leg in splints hanging heavily.

He could not go fast; he could not go
very far. Further inland, foggy gorse gave
place to broom and blighted bracken, all wet,
sagging with rain. Then he crossed a swale
of brown reeds and tussock set with little
pools of water, opaque and grey in the rain.

Where the outer moors narrowed he turned
westward; then a strip of low, thorn-clad
cliff confronted him, up which he toiled along
a V-shaped cleft choked with ferns.

The spectral forest of Läis lay just beyond, its wind-tortured branches tossing under
a leaden sky.

East and west lonely moors stretched away
into the depths of the mist; southward spread
the sea; to the north lay the wide woods of
Läis, equally deserted now in this sad and
empty land.

He hobbled to the edge of the forest and
stood knee deep in discoloured ferns, listening. The sombre beech-woods spread thick
on either hand, a wilderness of crossed limbs
and meshed branches to which still clung
great clots of dull brown leaves.

He listened, peering into sinister, grey

depths. In the uncertain light nothing stirred except the clashing branches overhead; there was no sound except the wind's flowing roar and the ghostly noise of his own voice, hallooing through the solitude—a voice in the misty void that seemed to carry less sound than the straining cry of a sleeper in his dreams.

If the aëroplane had landed, there was no sign here. How far had it struggled on, sheering the tree-tops, before it fell?—if indeed it had fallen somewhere in the wood's grey depths?

As long as he had sufficient strength he prowled along the forest, entering it here and there, calling, listening, searching the foggy corridors of trees. The rotting brake crackled underfoot; the tree tops clashed and creaked above him.

At last, having only enough strength left to take him home, he turned away, limping through the blotched and broken ferns, his crippled leg hanging stiffly in its splints, his gun and the dead ducks bobbing on his back.

The trodden way was soggy with little pools full of drenched grasses and dead leaves; but at length came rising ground, and the blue-green, glimmering wastes of gorse stretching away before him through the curtained fog.

A sheep path ran through; and after a little while a few trees loomed shadowy in the mist, and a low stone house took shape, whitewashed, flanked by barn, pigpen, and a stack of rotting seaweed.

A few wet hens wandered aimlessly by the doorstep; a tiny bed of white clove-pinks and tall white phlox exhaled a homely welcome as the lame man hobbled up the steps, pulled the leather latchstring, and entered.

In the kitchen an old Breton woman, chopping herbs, looked up at him out of aged eyes, shaking her head under its white coiffe.

"It is nearly noon," she said. "You have been out since dawn. Was it wise, for a convalescent, Monsieur Jacques?"

"Very wise, Marie-Josephine. Because the more exercise I take the sooner I shall be able to go back."

"It is too soon to go out in such weather."

"Ducks fly inland only in such weather,"

he retorted, smiling. "And we like roast widgeon, you and I, Marie-Josephine."

And all the while her aged blue eyes were fixed on him, and over her withered cheeks the soft bloom came and faded—that pretty colour which Breton women usually retain until the end.

"Thou knowest, Monsieur Jacques," she said, with a curiously quaint mingling of familiarity and respect, "that I do not counsel caution because I love thee and dread for thee again the trenches. But with thy leg hanging there like the broken wing of a *vanneau*——"

He replied good humouredly:

"Thou dost not know the Legion, Marie-Josephine. Every day in our trenches we break a comrade into pieces and glue him together again, just to make him tougher. Broken bones, once mended, are stronger than before."

He was looking down at her where she sat by the hearth, slicing vegetables and herbs, but watching him all the while out of her lovely, faded eyes.

"I understand, Monsieur Jacques, that you are like your father—God knows he was hardy and without fear—to the last"—she dropped her head—"Mary, glorious—intercede—" she muttered over her bowl of herbs.

Wayland, resting on his crutches, unslung his ducks, laid them on the table, smoothed their beautiful heads and breasts, then slipped the soaking *bandoulière* of his gun from his shoulder and placed the dripping piece against the chimney corner.

"After I have scrubbed myself," he said, "and have put on dry clothes, I shall come to luncheon; and I shall have something very strange to tell you, Marie-Josephine."

He limped away into one of the two remaining rooms—the other was hers—and closed his door.

Marie-Josephine continued to prepare the soup. There was an egg for him, too; and a slice of cold pork and a *brioche* and a jug of cider.

In his room Wayland was whistling "Tipperary."

Now and again, pausing in her work, she

turned her eyes to his closed door—wonderful eyes that became miracles of tenderness as she listened.

He came out, presently, dressed in his odd, ill-fitting uniform of the Legion, tunic unbuttoned, collarless of shirt, his bright, thick hair, now of decent length, in boyish disorder.

Delicious odours of soup and of Breton cider greeted him; he seated himself; Marie-Josephine waited on him, hovered over him, tucked a sack of feathers under his maimed leg, placed his crutches in the corner beside the gun.

Still eating, leisurely, he began:

"Marie-Josephine — a strange thing has happened on Quesnel Moors which troubles me. . . . Listen attentively. It was while waiting for ducks on the Eryx Rocks, that once I thought I heard through the roar of wind and sea the sound of a far cannonading. But I said to myself that it was only the imagination of a haunted mind; that in my ears still thundered the cannonade of Lens."

"Was it nevertheless true?" She had turned around from the fire where her own soup simmered in the kettle. As she spoke again she rose and came to the table.

He said: "It must have been cannon that I heard. Because, not long afterward, out of the fog came a great aëroplane rushing inland from the sea—flying swiftly above me —right over me!—and staggering like a wounded duck—it had one aileron broken— and sheered away into the fog, northward, Marie-Josephine."

Her work-worn hands, tightly clenched, rested now on the table and she leaned there, looking down at him.

"Was it an enemy—this airship, Jacques?"

"In the mist flying and the ragged clouds I could not tell. It might have been English. It must have been, I think—coming as it came from the sea. But I am troubled, Marie-Josephine. Were the guns at sea an enemy's guns? Did the aëroplane come to earth in safety? Where? In the Forest of Laïs? I found no trace of it."

She said, tremulous perhaps from standing too long motionless and intent:

"Is it possible that the Boches would come into these solitary moors, where there are no people any more, only the creatures of the Laïs woods, and the curlew and the lapwings which pass at evening?"

He ate thoughtfully and in silence for a while; then:

"They go, usually — the Boches — where there is plunder—murder to be done. . . . Spying to be done. . . . God knows what purpose animates the Huns. . . . After all, Lorient is not so far away. . . . Yet it surely must have been an English aëroplane, beaten off by some enemy ship—a submarine perhaps. God send that the rocks of the Isle des Chouans take care of her—with their teeth!"

He drank his cider—a sip or two only— then, setting aside the glass:

"I went from the Rocks of Eryx to Laïs Woods. I called as loudly as I could; the wind whirled my voice back into my throat. . . . I am not yet very strong. . . .

"Then I went into the wood as far as my strength permitted. I heard and saw nothing, Marie-Josephine."

"Would they be dead?" she asked.

"They were planing to earth. I don't know how much control they had, whether they could steer—choose a landing place. There are plenty of safe places on these moors."

"If their airship is crippled, what can they do, these English flying men, out there on the moors in the rain and wind? When the coast guard passes we must tell him."

"After lunch I shall go out again as far as my strength allows. . . . If the rain would cease and the mist lift, one might see something—be of some use, perhaps——"

"Ought you to go, Monsieur Jacques?"

"Could I fail to try to find them—Englishmen—and perhaps injured? Surely I should go, Marie-Josephine."

"The coast guard——"

"He passed the Eryx Rocks at daylight. He is at Sainte-Ylva now. Tonight, when I see his comrade's lantern, I shall stop him and report. But in the meanwhile I must go out and search."

"Spare thyself—for the trenches, Jacques. Remain indoors today." She began to unpin the coiffe which she always wore ceremoniously at meals when he was present.

He smiled: "Thou knowest I must go, Marie-Josephine."

"And if thou come upon them in the forest and they are Huns?"

He laughed: "They are English, I tell thee, Marie-Josephine!"

She nodded; under her breath, staring at the rain-lashed window: "Like thy father, thou must go forth," she muttered; "go always where thy spirit calls. And once *he* went. And came no more. 'And God help us all in Finistère, where all are born to grief."

CHAPTER VII

She had seated herself on a stool by the
hearth. Presently she spread her apron with
trembling fingers, took the glazed bowl of
soup upon her lap and began to eat, slowly,
casting long, unquiet glances at him from
time to time where he still at table leaned
heavily, looking out into the rain.

When he caught her eye he smiled, summoning her with a nod of his boyish head.
She set aside her bowl obediently, and, rising,
brought him his crutches. And at the same
moment somebody knocked lightly on the
outer door.

Marie-Josephine had unpinned her coiffe.
Now she pinned it on over her *bonnet* before
going to the door, glancing uneasily around
at him while she tied her tresses and settled

the delicate starched wings of her bonnet.

"That's odd," he said, "that knocking," staring at the door. "Perhaps it is the lost Englishman."

"God send them," she whispered, going to the door and opening it.

It certainly seemed to be one of the lost Englishmen—a big, square-shouldered, blond young fellow, tall and powerful, in the leather dress of an aëronaut. His glass mask was lifted like the visor of a tilting helmet, disclosing a red, weather-beaten face, wet with rain. Strength, youth, rugged health was their first impression of this leather-clad man from the clouds.

He stepped inside the house immediately, halted when he caught sight of Wayland in his undress uniform, glanced involuntarily at his crutches and bandaged leg, cast a quick, penetrating glance right and left; then he spoke pleasantly in his hesitating, imperfect French—so oddly imperfect that Wayland could not understand him at all.

"Who are you?" he demanded in English.

The airman seemed astonished for an instant, then a quick smile broke out on his ruddy features:

"I say, this *is* lucky! Fancy finding an Englishman here!—wherever this place may be." He laughed. "Of course I know I'm 'somewhere in France,' as the censor has it, but I'm hanged if I know where!"

"Come in and shut the door," said Wayland, reassured. Marie-Josephine closed the door. The aëronaut came forward, stood dripping a moment, then took the chair to which Wayland pointed, seating himself as though a trifle tired.

"Shot down," he explained, gaily. "An enemy submarine winged us out yonder somewhere. I tramped over these bally moors for hours before I found a sign of any path. A sheepwalk brought me here."

"You are lucky. There is only one house on these moors—this! Who are you?" asked Wayland.

"West—flight-lieutenant, 10th division, Cinque-Ports patrolling squadron."

"Good heavens, man! What are you doing in Finistère?"

"*What!*"

"You are in Brittany, province of Finistère. Didn't you know it?"

The air-officer seemed astounded. Presently he said: "The dirty weather foxed us. Then that fellow out yonder winged us. I was glad enough to see a coast line."

"Did you fall?"

"No; we controlled our landing pretty well."

"Where did you land?"

There was a second's hesitation; the airman looked at Wayland, glanced at his crippled leg.

"Out there near some woods," he said. "My pilot's there now trying to patch up. . . . You are not French, are you?"

"American."

"Oh! A—volunteer, I presume."

"Foreign Legion—2d."

"I see. Back from the trenches with a leg."

"It's nearly well. I'll be back soon."

"Can you walk?" asked the airman so

abruptly that Wayland, looking at him, hesitated, he did not quite know why.

"Not very far," he replied, cautiously. "I can get to the window with my crutches pretty well."

And the next moment he felt ashamed of his caution when the airman laughed frankly.

"I need a guide to some petrol," he said. "Evidently you can't go with me."

"Haven't you enough petrol to take you to Lorient?"

"How far is Lorient?"

Wayland told him.

"I don't know," said the flight-lieutenant; "I'll have to try to get somewhere. I suppose it is useless for me to ask," he added, "but have you, by any chance, a bit of canvas—an old sail or hammock?—I don't need much. That's what I came for—and some shellac and wire, and a screwdriver of sorts? We need patching as well as petrol; and we're a little short of supplies."

Wayland's steady gaze never left him, but his smile was friendly.

"We're in a tearing hurry, too," added the

flight-lieutenant, looking out of the window.

Wayland smiled. "Of course there's no petrol here. There's nothing here. I don't suppose you could have landed in a more deserted region if you had tried. There's a château in the Laïs woods, but it's closed; owner and servants are at the war and the family in Paris."

He shrugged his shoulders. "Everybody has cleared out; the war has stripped the country; and there never were any people on these moors, excepting shooting parties and, in the summer, a stray artist or two from Quimperlé."

The lieutenant looked at him. "You say there is nobody here—between here and Lorient? No—troops?"

"There's nothing to guard. The coast is one vast shoal. Ships pass hull down. Once a day a coast guard patrols along the cliffs——"

"When?"

"He has passed, unfortunately. Otherwise he might signal by relay to Lorient and have them send you out some petrol. By the way —are you hungry?"

The flight-lieutenant showed all his firm, white teeth under a yellow mustache, which curled somewhat upward. He laughed in a carefree way, as though something had suddenly eased his mind of perplexity—perhaps the certainty that there was no possible chance for petrol. Certainty is said to be more endurable than suspense.

"I'll stop for a bite—if you don't mind— while my pilot tinkers out yonder," he said. "We're not in such a bad way. It might easily have been worse. Do you think you could find us a bit of sail, or something, to use for patching?"

Wayland indicated an old high-backed chair of oak, quaintly embellished with ancient leather in faded blue and gold. It had been a royal chair in its day, or the Fleur-de-Lys lied.

The flight-lieutenant seated himself with a rather stiff bow.

"If you need canvas"—Wayland hesitated —then, gravely: "There are, in my room, a number of artists' *toiles*—old chassis with the blank canvas still untouched."

"Exactly what we need!" exclaimed the other. "What luck, now, to meet a painter in such a place as this!"

"They belonged to my father," explained Wayland. "We—Marie-Josephine and I—have always kept my father's old canvases and colours—everything of his. . . . I'll be glad to give them to a British soldier. . . . They're about all I have that was his—except that oak chair you sit on."

He rose on his crutches, spoke briefly in Breton to Marie-Josephine, then limped slowly away to his room.

When he returned with half a dozen blank canvases the flight-lieutenant, at table, was eating pork and black bread and drinking Breton cider.

Wayland seated himself, laid both crutches across his knees, picked up one of the chassis, and began to rip from it the dusty canvas. It was like tearing muscles from his own bones. But he smiled and chatted on, casually, with the air-officer, who ate as though half starved.

"I suppose," said Wayland, "you'll start

back across the Channel as soon as you secure petrol enough?"

"Yes, of course."

"You could go by way of Quimper or by Lorient. There's petrol to be had at both places for military purposes"—leisurely continuing to rip the big squares of canvas from the frames.

The airman, still eating, watched him askance at intervals.

"I've brought what's left of the shellac; it isn't much use, I fear. But here is his hammer and canvas stretcher, and the remainder of the nails he used for stretching his canvases," said Wayland, with an effort to speak carelessly.

"Many thanks. You also are a painter, I take it."

Wayland laid one hand on the sleeve of his uniform and laughed.

"I *was* a writer. But there are only soldiers in the world now."

"Quite so. . . . This is an odd place for an American to live in."

"My father bought it years ago. He was

a painter of peasant life." He added, lowering his voice, although Marie-Josephine understood no English: "This old peasant woman was his model many years ago. She also kept house for him. He lived here; I was born here."

"Really?"

"Yes, but my father desired that I grow up a good Yankee. I was at school in America when he—died."

The airman continued to eat very busily.

"He died—out there"—Wayland looked through the window, musingly. "There was an Iceland schooner wrecked off the Isle des Chouans. And no life-saving crew short of Ylva Light. So my father went out in his little American catboat, all alone. . . . Marie-Josephine saw his sail off Eryx Rocks . . . for a few moments . . . and saw it no more."

The airman, still devouring his bread and meat, nodded in silence.

"That is how it happened," said Wayland. "The French authorities notified me. There was a little money and this hut, and—Marie-Josephine. So I came here; and I write

children's stories—that sort of thing. . . .
It goes well enough. I sell a few to American publishers. Otherwise I shoot and fish
and read . . . when war does not preoccupy
me. . . ."

He smiled, experiencing the vague relief of
talking to somebody in his native tongue.
Quesnel Moors were sometimes very lonely.

"It's been a long convalescence," he continued, smilingly. "One of their 'coal-boxes'
did this"—touching his leg. "When I was
able to move I went to America. But the sea
off the Eryx called me back; and the authorities permitted me to come down here. I'm
getting well very fast now."

He had stripped every chassis of its canvas, and had made a roll of the material.

"I'm very glad to be of any use to you,"
he said pleasantly, laying the roll on the
table.

Marie-Josephine, on her low chair by the
hearth, sat listening to every word as though
she had understood. The expression in her
faded eyes varied constantly; solicitude, perplexity, vague uneasiness, a recurrent glim-

mer of suspicion were succeeded always by wistful tenderness when her gaze returned to Wayland and rested on his youthful face and figure with a pride forever new.

Once she spoke in mixed French and Breton:

"Is the stranger English, Monsieur Jacques, *mon cheri?*"

"I do not doubt it, Marie-Josephine. Do you?"

"Why dost thou believe him to be English?"

"He has the tricks of speech. Also his accent is of an English university. There is no mistaking it."

"Are not young Huns sometimes instructed in the universities of England?"

"Yes. . . . But——"

"*Gar à nous, mon p'tit,* Jacques. In Finistère a stranger is a suspect. Since earliest times they have done us harm in Finistère. The strangers—God knows what centuries of evil they have wrought."

"No fear," he said, reassuringly, and turned again to the airman, who had now satisfied his hunger and had already risen to gather up the roll of canvas, the hammer, nails, and shellac.

"Thanks awfully, old chap!" he said cordially. "I'll take these articles, if I may. It's very good of you. . . . I'm in a tearing hurry——"

"Won't your pilot come over and eat a bit?"

"I'll take him this bread and meat, if I may. Many thanks." He held out his heavily gloved hand with a friendly smile, nodded to Marie-Josephine. And as he hurriedly turned to go, the ancient carving on the high-backed chair caught him between the buttons of his leather coat, tearing it wide open over the breast. And Wayland saw the ribbon of the Iron Cross there fastened to a sea-grey tunic.

There was a second's frightful silence.

"What's that you wear?" said Wayland hoarsely. "Stop! Stand where you——"

"Halt! Don't touch that shotgun!" cried the airman sharply. But Wayland already had it in his hands, and the airman fired twice at him where he stood—steadied the automatic to shoot again, but held his fire, seeing it would not be necessary. Besides, he did not care to shoot the old woman unless military precaution made it advisable; and she was on her knees, her withered arms upflung, shielding the prostrate body with her own.

"You Yankee fool," he snapped out harshly—"it is your own fault, not mine! . . . Like the rest of your imbecile nation you poke your nose where it has no business! And I—" He ceased speaking, realizing that his words remained unheard.

After a moment he backed toward the door, carrying the canvas roll under his left arm and keeping his eye carefully on the prostrate man. Also, one can never trust the French!—he was quite ready for that old woman there on the floor who was holding the dead boy's head to her breast, muttering: "My darling! My child!—Oh, little son of Marie-Josephine!—I told thee—I warned thee of the stranger in Finistère! . . . Marie — holy — intercede! . . . All — all are born to grief in Finistère! . . ."

CHAPTER VIII

The incredible rumour that German airmen were in Brittany first came from Plouharnel in Morbihan; then from Bannalec, where an old Icelander had notified the Brigadier of the local Gendarmerie. But the Icelander was very drunk. A thimble of cognac did it.

Again came an unconfirmed report that a shepherd lad while alternately playing on his Biniou and fishing for eels at the confluence of the Elle and Isole, had seen a werewolf in Laïs Woods. The Loup Garou walked on two legs and had assumed the shape of a man with no features except two enormous eyes.

The following week a coast guard near Flouranges telephoned to the Aulnes Light-

92

house; the keeper of the light telephoned to Lorient the story of Wayland, and was instructed to extinguish the great flash again and to keep watch from the lantern until an investigation could be made.

That an enemy airman had done murder in Finistère was now certain; but that a Boche submarine had come into the Bay of Biscay seemed very improbable, considering the measures which had been taken in the Channel, at Trieste, and at Gibraltar.

That a fleet of many sea-planes was soaring somewhere between the Isle des Chouettes and Finistère, and landing men, seemed to be practically an impossibility. Yet, there were the rumours. And murder had been done.

But an enemy undersea boat required a base. Had such a base been established somewhere along those lonely and desolate wastes of bog and rock and moor and gorse-set cliff haunted only by curlew and wild duck, and bounded inland by a silent barrier of forest through which the wild boar roamed and rooted unmolested?

And where in Finistère was an enemy sea-plane to come from, when, save for the few remaining submarines still skulking near British waters, the enemy's flag had vanished from the seas?

Nevertheless the coast lights at Aulnes and on the Isle des Chouettes went out; the Commandant at Lorient and the General in command of the British expeditionary troops in the harbour consulted; and the fleet of troop-laden transports did not sail as scheduled, but a swarm of French and British cruisers, trawlers, mine-sweepers, destroyers, and submarines put out from the great warport to comb the boisterous seas of Biscay for any possible aërial or amphibious Hun who might venture to haunt the coasts.

Inland, too, officers were sent hither and thither to investigate various rumours and doubtful reports at their several sources.

And it happened in that way that Captain Neeland of the 6th Battalion, Athabasca Regiment, Canadian Overseas Contingent, found himself in the Forest of Aulnes, with instructions to stay there long enough to verify or discredit a disturbing report which had just arrived by mail.

The report was so strange and the investigation required so much secrecy and caution that Captain Neeland changed his uniform for knickerbockers and shooting coat, borrowed a fowling piece and a sack of cartridges loaded with No. 4 shot, tucked his gun under his arm, and sauntered out of Lorient town before dawn, like any other duck-hunting enthusiast.

Several reasons influenced his superiors in sending Neeland to investigate this latest and oddest report: for one thing, although he had become temporarily a Canadian for military purposes only, in reality he was an American artist who, like scores and scores of his artistic fellow Yankees, had spent many years industriously painting those sentimental Breton scenes which obsess our painters, if not their critics. He was a very bad painter, but he did not know it; he had already become a promising soldier, but he did not realize that either. As a sportsman, however, Neeland was rather pleased with himself.

He was sent because he knew the sombre and lovely land of Finistère pretty well, because he was more or less of a naturalist and a sportsman, and because the plan which he had immediately proposed appeared to be reasonable as well as original.

It had been a stiff walk across country —fifteen miles, as against thirty odd around by road—but neither cart nor motor was to enter into the affair. If anybody should watch him, he was only a duckhunter afield, crossing the marshes, skirting *étangs*, a solitary figure in the waste, easily reconcilable with his wide and melancholy surroundings.

CHAPTER IX

L'OMBRE

Aulnes Woods were brown and still under their unshed canopy of October leaves. Against a grey, transparent sky the oaks and beeches towered, unstirred by any wind; in the subdued light among the trees, ferns, startlingly green, spread delicate plumed fronds; there was no sound except the soft crash of his own footsteps through shriveling patches of brake; no movement save when a yellow leaf fluttered down from above or one of those little silvery grey moths took wing and fluttered aimlessly along the forest aisle, only to alight upon some lichen-spotted tree and cling there, slowly waving its delicate, translucent wings.

It was a very ancient wood, the Forest of Aulnes, and the old trees were long past timber value. Even those gleaners of dead wood and fallen branches seemed to have passed a different way, for the forest floor was littered with material that seldom goes to waste in Europe, and which broke under foot with a dull, thick sound, filling the nostrils with the acrid odour of decay.

Narrow paths full of dead leaves ran here and there through the woods, but he took none of these, keeping straight on toward the northwest until a high, moss-grown wall checked his progress.

It ran west through the silent forest; damp green mould and lichens stained it; patches of grey stucco had peeled from it, revealing underneath the roughly dressed stones. He followed the wall.

Now and then, far in the forest, and indistinctly, he heard faint sounds—perhaps the cautious tread of roebuck, or rabbits in the bracken, or the patter of a stoat over dry leaves; perhaps the sullen retirement of some wild boar, winding man in the depths of his own domain, and sulkily conceding him right of way.

After a while there came a break in the wall where four great posts of stone stood, and where there should have been gates.

But only the ancient and rusting hinges remained of either gate or wicket.

He looked up at the carved escutcheons; the moss of many centuries had softened and smothered the sculptured device, so that its form had become indistinguishable.

Inside stood a stone lodge. Tiles had fallen from the ancient roof; leaded panes were broken; nobody came to the closed and discoloured door of massive oak.

The avenue, which was merely an unkempt, overgrown ride, curved away between the great gateposts into the woods; and, as he entered it, three deer left stealthily, making no sound in the forest.

Nobody was to be seen, neither gatekeeper nor woodchopper nor charcoal burner. Nothing moved amid the trees except a tiny, silent bird belated in his autumn migration.

The ride curved to the east; and abruptly he came into view of the house—a low, weather-ravaged structure in the grassy glade, ringed by a square, wet moat.

There was no terrace; the ride crossed a permanent bridge of stone, passed the carved and massive entrance, crossed a second crumbling causeway, and continued on into the forest.

An old Breton woman, who was drawing a jug of water from the moat, turned and looked at Neeland, and then went silently into the house.

A moment later a younger woman appeared on the doorstep and stood watching his approach.

As he crossed the bridge he took off his cap.

"Madame, the Countess of Aulnes?" he inquired. "Would you be kind enough to say to her that I arrive from Lorient at her request?"

"I am the Countess of Aulnes," she said in flawless English.

He bowed again. "I am Captain Neeland of the British Expeditionary force."

"May I see your credentials, Captain Neeland?" She had descended the single step of crumbling stone.

"Pardon, Countess; may I first be certain concerning *your* identity?"

There was a silence. To Neeland she seemed very young in her black gown. Perhaps it was that sombre setting and her dark eyes and hair which made her skin seem so white.

"What proof of my identity do you expect?" she asked in a low voice.

"Only one word, Madame."

She moved a step nearer, bent a trifle toward him. "L'Ombre," she whispered.

From his pocket he drew his credentials and offered them. Among them was her own letter to the authorities at Lorient.

After she had examined them she handed them back to him.

"Will you come in, Captain Neeland—or, perhaps we had better seat ourselves on the bridge—in order to lose no time—because I wish you to see for yourself——"

She lifted her dark eyes; a tint of embarrassment came into her cheeks: "It may seem

absurd to you; it seems so to me, at times—
what I am going to say to you—concerning
L'Ombre——"

She had turned; he followed; and at her
grave gesture of invitation, he seated himself beside her on the coping of mossy stone
which ran like a bench under the parapet of
the little bridge.

"Captain Neeland," she said, "I am a Bretonne, but, until recently, I did not suppose
myself to be superstitious. . . . I really am
not—unless—except for this one matter of
L'Ombre. . . . My English governess drove
superstition out of my head. . . . Still, living
in Finistère—here in this house"—she flushed
again—"I shall have to leave it to you. . . .
I dread ridicule; but I am sure you are too
courteous— . . . It required some courage
for me to write to Lorient. But, if it might
possibly help my country—to risk ridicule—
of course I do not hesitate."

She looked uncertainly at the young man's
pleasant, serious face, and, as though reassured:

"I shall have to tell you a little about

myself first—so that you may understand better."

"Please," he said gravely.

"Then—my father and my only brother died a year ago, in battle. . . . It happened in the Argonne. . . . I am alone. We had maintained only two men servants here. They went with their classes. One old woman remains." She looked up with a forced smile. "I need not explain to you that our circumstances are much straitened. You have only to look about you to see that . . . our poverty is not recent; it always has been so within my memory—only growing a little worse every year. I believe our misfortunes began during the Vendée. . . . But that is of no interest . . . except that—through coincidence, of course—every time a new misfortune comes upon our family, misfortune also falls on France." He nodded, still mystified, but interested.

"Did you happen to notice the device carved on the gatepost?" she asked.

"I thought it resembled a fish——"

"Do you understand French, Captain Neeland?"

"Yes."

"Then you know that L'Ombre means 'the shadow'."

"Yes."

"Did you know, also, that there is a fish called 'L'Ombre'?"

"No; I did not know that."

"There is. It looks like a shadow in the water. L'Ombre does not belong here in Brittany. It is a northern fish of high altitudes where waters are icy and rapid and always tinctured with melted snow . . . would you accord me a little more patience, Monsieur, if I seem to be garrulous concerning my own family? It is merely because I want you to understand everything . . . *everything*. . . ."

"I am interested," he assured her pleasantly.

"Then—it is a legend—perhaps a superstition in our family—that any misfortune to us—*and to France*—is always preceded by two invariable omens. One of these dreaded signs is the abrupt appearance of L'Ombre in the

104

waters of our moat—" She turned her head slowly and looked down over the parapet of the bridge.—"The other omen," she continued quietly, "is that the clocks in our house suddenly go wrong—all striking the same hour, no matter where the hands point, no matter what time it really is. . . . These things have always happened in our family, they say. I, myself, have never before witnessed them. But during the Vendée the clocks persisted in striking four times every hour. The Comte d'Aulnes mounted the scaffold at that hour; the Vicomte died under Charette at Fontenay at that hour. . . . L'Ombre appeared in the waters of the moat at four o'clock one afternoon. And then the clocks went wrong.

"And all this happened again, they say, in 1870. L'Ombre appeared in the moat. Every clock continued to strike six, day after day for a whole week, until the battle of Sedan ended. . . . My grandfather died there with the light cavalry. . . . I am so afraid I am taxing your courtesy, Captain Neeland——"

"I am intensely interested," he repeated,

watching the lovely, sensitive face which pride and dread of misinterpretation had slightly flushed again.

"It is only to explain—perhaps to justify myself for writing—for asking that an officer be sent here from Lorient for a few days——"

"I understand, Countess."

"Thank you. . . . Had it been merely for myself—for my own fears—my personal safety, I should not have written. But our misfortunes seem to be coincident with my country's mishaps. . . . So I thought—if they sent an officer who would be kind enough to understand——"

"I understand . . . L'Ombre has appeared in the moat again, has it not?"

"Yes, it came a week ago, suddenly, at five o'clock in the afternoon."

"And—the clocks?"

"For a week they have been all wrong."

"What hour do they strike?" he asked curiously.

"Five."

"No matter where the hands point?"

"No matter. I have tried to regulate them.

I have done everything I could do. But they continue to strike five every hour of the day and night. . . . I have"—a pale smile touched her lips—"I have been a little wakeful—perhaps a trifle uneasy—on my country's account. You understand. . . ." Pride and courage had permitted her no more than uneasiness, it seemed. Or if fear had threatened her there in her lonely bedroom through the still watches of the night, she desired him to understand that her solicitude was for France, not for any daughter of the race whose name she bore.

The simplicity and directness of her amazing narrative had held his respect and attention; there could be no doubt that she implicitly believed what she told him.

But that was one thing; and the wild extravagance of the story was another. There must be, of course, an explanation for these phenomena other than a supernatural one. Such things do not happen except in medieval romance and tales of sorcery and doom. And of all regions on earth Brittany swarms with such tales and superstitions. He knew it.

And this young girl was Bretonne after all, however educated, however accomplished, however honest and modern and sincere. And he began to comprehend that the germs of superstition and credulity were in the blood of every Breton ever born.

But he merely said with pleasant deference: "I can very easily understand your uneasiness and perplexity, Madame. It is a time of mental stress, of great nervous tension in France—of heart-racking suspense——"

She lifted her dark eyes. "You do not believe me, Monsieur."

"I believe what you have told me. But I believe, also, that there is a natural explanation concerning these matters."

"I tell myself so, too. . . . But I brood over them in vain; I can find no explanation."

"Of course there must be one," he insisted carelessly. "Is there anything in the world more likely to go queer than a clock?"

"There are five clocks in the house. Why should they all go wrong at the same time and in the same manner?"

He smiled. "I don't know," he said frankly.

"I'll investigate, if you will permit me."

"Of course. . . . And, about L'Ombre. What could explain its presence in the moat? It is a creature of icy waters; it is extremely limited in its range. My father has often said that, except L'Ombre which has appeared at long intervals in our moat, L'Ombre never has been seen in Brittany."

"From where does this clear water come which fills the moat?" he asked, smiling.

"From living springs in the bottom."

"No doubt," he said cheerfully, "a long subterranean vein of water connects these springs with some distant Alpine river, somewhere—in the Pyrenees, perhaps—" He hesitated, for the explanation seemed as far-fetched as the water.

Perhaps it so appeared to her, for she remained politely silent.

Suddenly, in the house, a clock struck five times. They both sat listening intently. From the depths of the ancient mansion, the other clocks repeated the strokes, first one, then another, then two sounding their clear little bells almost in unison. All struck five. He drew out his watch and looked at it. The hour was three in the afternoon.

After a moment her attitude, a trifle rigid, relaxed. He muttered something about making an examination of the clocks, adding that to adjust and regulate them would be a simple matter.

She sat very still beside him on the stone coping—her dark eyes wandered toward the forest—wonderful eyes, dreamily preoccupied —the visionary eyes of a Bretonne, full of the mystery and beauty of magic things unseen.

Venturing, at last, to disturb the delicate sequence of her thoughts: "Madame," he said, "have you heard any rumours concerning enemy airships—or, undersea boats?"

The tranquil gaze returned, rested on him: "No, but something has been happening in the Aulnes Etang."

"What?"

"I don't know. But every day the wild ducks rise from it in fright—clouds of them— and the curlew and lapwings fill the sky with their clamour."

"A poacher?"

"I know of none remaining here in Finistère."

"Have you seen anything in the sky? An eagle?"

"Only the wild fowl whirling above the *étang.*"

"You have heard nothing — from the clouds?"

"Only the *vanneaux* complaining and the wild curlew answering."

"Where is L'Ombre?" he asked, vaguely troubled.

She rose; he followed her across the bridge and along the mossy border of the moat. Presently she stood still and pointed down in silence.

For a while he saw nothing in the moat; then, suspended midway between surface and bottom, motionless in the transparent water, a shadow, hanging there, colourless, translucent —a phantom vaguely detached from the limpid element through which it loomed.

L'Ombre lay very still in the silvery-grey depths where the glass of the stream reflected the façade of that ancient house.

Around the angle of the moat crept a ripple; a rat appeared, swimming, and, seeing them, dived. L'Ombre never stirred.

An involuntary shudder passed over Neeland, and he looked up abruptly with the instinct of a creature suddenly trapped—but not yet quite realizing it.

In the grey forest walling that silent place, in the monotonous sky overhead, there seemed something indefinitely menacing; a menace, too, in the intense stillness; and, in the twisted, uplifted limbs of every giant tree, a subtle and suspended threat.

He said tritely and with an effort: "For everything there are natural causes. These may always be discovered with ingenuity and persistence. . . . Shall we examine your clocks, Madame?"

"Yes. . . . Will your General be annoyed because I have asked that an officer be sent here? Tell me truthfully, are *you* annoyed?"

"No, indeed," he insisted, striving to smile away the inexplicable sense of depression which was creeping over him.

He looked down again at the grey wraith

in the water, then, as they turned and walked slowly back across the bridge together, he said, suddenly:

"*Something* is wrong somewhere in Finistère. That is evident to me. There have been too many rumours from too many sources. By sea and land they come—rumours of things half seen, half heard—glimpses of enemy aircraft, sea-craft. Yet their presence would appear to be an impossibility in the light of the military intelligence which we possess.

"But we have investigated every rumour; although I, personally, know of no report which has been confirmed. Nevertheless, these rumours persist; they come thicker and faster day by day. But this—" He hesitated, then smiled—"this seems rather different——"

"I know. I realize that I have invited ridicule——"

"Countess——"

"You are too considerate to say so. . . . And perhaps I have become nervous—imagining things. It might easily be so. Perhaps it is the sadness of the past year—the strangeness of it, and——"

She sighed unconsciously.

"It is lonely in the Wood of Aulnes," she said.

"Indeed it must be very lonely here," he returned in a low voice.

"Yes. . . . Aulnes Wood is—too remote for them to send our wounded here for their convalescence. I offered Aulnes. Then I offered myself, saying that I was ready to go anywhere if I might be of use. It seems there are already too many volunteers. They take only the trained in hospitals. I am untrained, and they have no leisure to teach . . . nobody wanted me."

She turned and gazed dreamily at the forest.

"So there is nothing for me to do," she said, "except to remain here and sew for the hospitals." . . . She looked out thoughtfully across the fern-grown *carrefour:* "Therefore I sew all day by the latticed window there—all day long, day after day—and when one is young and when there is nobody—nothing to look at except the curlew flying—nothing to hear except the *vanneaux,* and the clocks striking the hour——"

Her voice had altered subtly, but she lifted her proud little head and smiled, and her tone grew firm again:

"You see, Monsieur, I am truly becoming a trifle morbid. It is entirely physical; my heart is quite undaunted."

"You heart, Madame, is but a part of the great, undaunted heart of France."

"Yes . . . therefore there could be no fear —no doubt of God. . . . Affairs go well with France, Monsieur?—may I ask without military impropriety?"

"France, as always, faces her destiny, Madame. And her destiny is victory and light."

"Surely . . . I knew; only I had heard nothing for so long. . . . Thank you, Monsieur."

He said quietly: "The Light shall break. We must not doubt it, we English. Nor can you doubt the ultimate end of this vast and hellish Darkness which has been let loose upon the world to assail it. You shall live to see light, Madame—and I also shall see it—perhaps——"

She looked up at the young man, met his

eyes, and looked elsewhere, gravely. A slight flush lingered on her cheeks.

On the doorstep of the house they paused. "Is it possible," she asked, "that an enemy aëroplane could land in the Aulnes Étang?— L'Étang aux Vanneaux?"

"In the Étang?" he repeated, a little startled. "How large is it, this Étang aux Vanneaux?"

"It is a lake. It is perhaps a mile long and three-quarters of a mile across. My old servant, Anne, had seen the werewolf in the reeds—like a man without a face—and only two great eyes—" She forced a pale smile. "Of course, if it were anything she saw, it was a real man. . . . And, airmen dress that way. . . . I wondered——"

He stood looking at her absently, worrying his short mustache.

"One of the rumours we have heard," he began, "concerns a supposed invasion by a huge fleet of German battle-planes of enormous dimensions—a new biplane type which is steered from the bridge like an ocean steamer.

"It is supposed to be three or four times as large as their usual *Albatross* type, with a vast cruising radius, immense capacity for lifting, and powerful enough to carry a great weight of armour, equipment, munitions, and a very large crew.

"And the most disturbing thing about it is that it is said to be as noiseless as a high-class automobile."

"Has such an one been seen in Brittany?"

"Such a machine has been reported—many, many times—as though not one but hundreds were in Finistère. And, what is very disquieting to us—a report has arrived from a distant and totally independent source—from Sweden —that air-crafts of this general type have been secretly built in Germany by the hundreds."

After a moment's silence she stepped into the house; he followed.

The great, bare, grey rooms were in keeping with the grey exterior; age had more than softened and coördinated the ancient furnishings, it had rendered them colourless, without accent, making the place empty and monotonous.

Her chair and workbasket stood by a latticed window; she seated herself and took up her sewing, watching him where he stood before the fireplace fussing over a little mantel clock—a gilt and ebony affair of the consulate, shaped like a lyre, the pendulum being also the clock itself and containing the works, bell and dial.

When he had adjusted it to his satisfaction he tested it. It still struck five. He continued to fuss over it for half an hour, testing it at intervals, but it always struck five times, and finally he gave up his attempts with a shrug of annoyance.

"*I* can't do anything with it," he admitted, smiling cheerfully across the room at her; "is there another clock on this floor?"

She directed him; he went into an adjoining room where, on the mantel, a modern enamelled clock was ticking busily. But after a little while he gave up his tinkering; he could do nothing with it; the bell persistently struck five. He returned to where she sat sewing, admitting failure with a perplexed and uneasy smile; and she rose and accompanied him

118

through the house, where he tried, in turn, every one of the other clocks.

When, at length, he realized that he could accomplish nothing by altering their striking mechanism—that every clock in the house persisted in striking five times no matter where the hands were pointing, a sudden, odd, and inward rage possessed him to hurl the clocks at the wall and stamp the last vestiges of mechanism out of them.

As they returned together through the hushed and dusky house, he caught glimpses of faded and depressing tapestries; of vast, tarnished mirrors, through the dim depths of which their passing figures moved like ghosts; of rusted stands of arms, and armoured lay figures where cobwebs clotted the slitted visors and the frail tatters of ancient faded banners drooped.

And he understood why any woman might believe in strange inexplicable things here in the haunting stillness of this house where splendour had turned to mould—where form had become effaced and colour dimmed; where only

the shadowy film of texture still remained,
and where even that was slowly yielding—
under the attacks of Time's relentless mer-
cenaries, moth and dust and rust.

CHAPTER X

They dined by the latticed window; two candles lighted them; old Anne served them—old Anne of Fäouette in her wide white coiffe and collarette, her velvet bodice and her *chaussons* broidered with the rose.

Always she talked as she moved about with dish and salver—garrulous, deaf, and aged, and perhaps flushed with the gentle afterglow of that second infancy which comes before the night.

"*Ouidame!* It is I, Anne Le Bihan, who tell you this, my pretty gentleman. I have lived through eighty years and I have seen life begin and end in the Woods of Aulnes—alas! —in the Woods and the House of Aulnes——"

"The red wine, Anne," said her mistress, gently.

"Madame the Countess is served. . . . These grapes grew when I was young, Monsieur —and the world was young, too, *mon Capitaine—hélas!*—but the Woods of Aulnes were old, old as the headland yonder. Only the sea is older, *beau jeune homme*—only the sea is older—the sea which always was and will be."

"Madame," he said, turning toward the young girl beside him, "—to France!—I have the honour—" She touched her glass to his and they saluted France with the ancient wine of France—a sip, a faint smile, and silence through which their eyes still lingered for a moment.

"This year is yielding a bitter vintage," he said. "Light is lacking. But—but there will be sun enough another year."

"Yes."

"*B'en oui!* The sun must shine again," muttered old Anne, "but not in the Woods of Aulnes. *Non pas.* There is no sunlight in the Woods of Aulnes where all is dim and still; where the Blessed walk at dawn with

Our Lady of Aulnes in shining vestments all——"

"She has seen thin mists rising there," whispered the Countess in his ear.

"In shining robes of grace—*oui-da!*—the martyrs and the acolytes of God. It is I who tell you, *beau jeune homme*—I, Anne of Fä-ouette. I saw them pass where, on my two knees, I gathered orange mushrooms by the brook! I heard them singing prettily and loud, hymns of our blessed Lady——"

"She heard a throstle singing by the brook," whispered the châtelaine of Aulnes. Her breath was delicately fragrant on his cheek.

Against the grey dusk at the window she looked to him like a slim spirit returned to haunt the halls of Aulnes—some graceful shade come back out of the hazy and forgotten years of gallantry and courts and battles—the exquisite apparition of that golden time before the Vendée drowned and washed it out in blood.

"I am so glad you came," she said. "I have not felt so calm, so confident, in months."

Old Anne of Fäouette laid them fresh napkins and set two crystal bowls beside them and filled the bowls with fresh water from the moat.

"Ho fois!" she said, "love and the heart may change, but not the Woods of Aulnes; they never change—they never change. . . . The golden people of Ker-Ys come out of the sea to walk among the trees."

The Countess whispered: "She has seen the sunbeams slanting through the trees."

"Vrai, c'est moi, Anne Le Bihan, qui vous dites cela, mon Capitaine! And, in the Woods of Aulnes the werewolf prowls. I have seen him, gallant gentleman. He walks upright, and, in his head, he has only eyes; no mouth, no teeth, no nostrils, and no hair—the Loup-Garou!—O Lady of Aulnes, adored and blessed, protect us from the Loup-Barou!"

The Countess said again to him: "I have not felt so confident, so content, so full of faith in months——"

A far faint clamour came to their ears; high in the fading sky above the forest vast clouds of wild fowl rose like smoke, whirling, circling, swinging wide, drifting against the dying light of day, southward toward the sea.

"There is something wrong there," he said, under his breath.

Minute after minute they watched in silence. The last misty shred of wild fowl floated seaward and was lost against the clouds.

"Is there a path to the Étang?" he asked quietly.

"Yes. I will go with you——"

"No."

"Why?"

"No. Show me the path."

His shotgun stood by the door; he took it with him as he left the house beside her. In the moat, close by the bridge, and pointing toward the house, L'Ombre lay motionless. They saw it as they passed, but did not speak of it to each other. At the forest's edge he halted: "Is this the path?"

"Yes. . . . May I not go?"

"No—please."

"Is there danger?"

"No. . . . I don't know if there is any danger."

"Will you be cautious, then?"

He turned and looked at her in the dim light. Standing so for a little while they remained silent. Then he drew a deep, quiet breath. She held out one hand, slowly; half way he bent and touched her fingers with his lips; released them. Her arm fell listlessly at her side.

After he had been gone a long while, she turned away, moving with head lowered. At the bridge she waited for him.

A red moon rose low in the east. It became golden above the trees, paler higher, and deathly white in mid-heaven.

It was long after midnight when she went into the house to light fresh candles. In the intense darkness before dawn she lighted two more and set them in an upper window on the chance that they might guide him back.

At five in the morning every clock struck five.

She was not asleep; she was lying on a lounge beside the burning candles, listening, when the door below burst open and there came the trampling rush of feet, the sound of blows, a fall——

A loud voice cried:—"Because you are armed and not in uniform!—you British swine!"—

And the pistol shots crashed through the house.

On the stairs she swayed for an instant, grasped blindly at the rail. Through the floating smoke below the dead man lay there by the latticed window—where they had sat together—he and she——

Spectres were flitting to and fro—grey shapes without faces—things with eyes. A loud voice dinned in her ears, beat savagely upon her shrinking brain:

"You there on the stairs!—do you hear? What are those candles? Signals?"

She looked down at the dead man.

"Yes," she said.

Through the crackling racket of the fusillade, down, down into roaring darkness she fell.

After a few moments her slim hand moved, closed over the dead man's. And moved no more.

In the moat L'Ombre still remained, un-stirring; old Anne lay in the kitchen dying; and the Wood of Aulnes was swarming with ghastly shapes which had no faces, only eyes.

CHAPTER XI

It was Dr. Vail whose identification secured burial for Neeland, not in the American cemetery, but in Aulnes Wood.

When the raid into Finistère ended, and the unclean birds took flight, Vail, at Quimper, ordered north with his unit, heard of the tragedy, and went to Aulnes. And so Neeland was properly buried beside the youthful châtelaine. Which was, no doubt, what his severed soul desired. And perhaps hers desired it, too.

Vail continued on to Paris, to Flanders, got gassed, and came back to New York.

He had aged ten years in as many months.

Gray, the younger surgeon, kept glancing from time to time at Vail's pallid face, and the latter understood the professional interest of the younger man.

"You think I look ill?" he asked, finally.

"You don't look very fit, Doctor."

"No. . . . I'm *going West.*"

"You mean it?"

"Yes."

"Why do you think that you are—*going West?*"

"There's a thing over there, born of gas. It's a living thing, animal or vegetable. I don't know which. It's only recently been recognized. We call it the 'Seed of Death.'"

Gray gazed at the haggard face of the older man in silence.

Vail went on, slowly: "It's properly named. It is always fatal. A man may live for a few months. But, once gassed, even in the slightest degree, if that germ is inhaled, death is certain."

After a silence Gray began: "Do you have any apprehension—" And did not finish the sentence.

Vail shrugged. "It's interesting, isn't it?" he said with pleasant impersonality.

After a silence Gray said: "Are you doing anything about it?"

"Oh, yes. It's working in the dark, of course. I'm feeling rottener every day."

He rested his handsome head on one thin hand:

"I don't want to die, Gray, but I don't know how to keep alive. It's odd, isn't it? I don't wish to die. It's an interesting world. I want to see how the local elections turn out in New York."

"What!"

"Certainly. That is what worries me more than anything. We Allies are sure to win. I'm not worrying about that. But I'd like to live to see Tammany a dead cock in the pit!"

Gray forced a laugh; Vail laughed unfeignedly, and then, solemn again, said:

"I'd like to live to see this country aspire to something really noble."

"After all," said Gray, "there is really nothing to stifle aspiration."

It was not only because Vail had been gazing upon death in every phase, every degree— on brutal destruction wholesale and in detail; but also he had been standing on the outer escarpment of Civilization and had watched the mounting sea of barbarism battering, thundering, undermining, gradually engulfing the world itself and all its ancient liberties.

He and the young surgeon, Gray, who was to sail to France next day were alone together on the loggia of the club; dusk mitigated the infernal heat of a summer day in town.

On the avenue below motor cars moved north and south, hansoms crept slowly along the curb, and on the hot sidewalks people passed listlessly under the electric lights—the nine—and—seventy sweating tribes.

For, on such summer nights, under the red moon, an exodus from the East Side peoples the noble avenue with dingy spectres who shuffle along the gilded grilles and still façades of stone, up and down, to and fro, in quest of God knows what—of air perhaps, perhaps of happiness, or of something even vaguer. But whatever it may be that starts them into painful motion, one thing seems certain: aspiration is a part of their unrest.

"There is liberty here," replied Dr. Vail— "also her inevitable shadow, tyranny."

"We need more light; that's all," said Gray.

"When light streams in from every angle no shadow is possible."

"The millennium? I get you. . . . In this country the main thing is that there is *some* light. A single ray, however feeble, and even coming from one fixed angle only, means aspiration, life. . . ."

He lighted a cigar.

"As you know," he remarked, "there is a flower called *Aconitum*. It is also known by the ominous names of Monks-Hood and Helmet-Flower. Direct sunlight kills it. It flourishes only in shadow. Like the Kaiser-Flower it also is blue; and," he added, "it is deadly poison. . . . As you say, the necessary thing in this world is light from every angle."

His cigar glimmered dully through the silence. Presently he went on; "Speaking of tyranny, I think it may be classed as a recognized and tolerated business carried on successfully by those born with a genius for it. It flourishes in the shade—like the Helmet-Flower. . . . But the sun in this Western Hemisphere of ours is devilish hot. It's gradually killing off our local tyrants—slowly, almost imperceptiby but inexorably, killing 'em off. . . . Of course, there are plenty still alive —tyrants of every degree born to the business of tyranny and making a success at it."

He smoked tranquilly for a while, then:

"There are our tyrants of industry," he said; "tyrants of politics, tyrants of religion—great and small we still harbor plenty of tyrants, all scheming to keep their roots from shriveling under this fierce western sun of ours——"

He laughed without mirth, turning his worn and saddened eyes on Gray:

"Tyranny is a business," he repeated; "also it is a state of mind—a delusion, a ruling passion—strong even in death. . . . The odd part of it is that a tyrant never knows he's one. . . . He invariably mistakes himself for a local Moses. I can tell you a sort of story if you care to listen. . . . Or, we can go to some cheerful show or roof-garden——"

"Go on with your story," said Gray.

CHAPTER XII

Vail began:

Tyranny was purely a matter of business with this little moral shrimp about whom I'm going to tell you. I was standing between a communication trench and a crater left by a mine which was being "consolidated," as they have it in these days. . . . All around me soldiers of the third line swarmed and clambered over the débris, digging, hammering, shifting planks and sandbags from south to north, lugging new timbers, reels of barbed wire, ladders, cases of ammunition, machine guns, trench mortars.

The din of the guns was terrific; overhead our own shells passed with a deafening, clattering roar; the Huns continued to shell the town in front of us where our first and second lines were still fighting in the streets and houses while the third line were reconstructing a few yards of trenches and a few craters won.

Stretchers and bearers from my section had not yet returned from the emergency dressing station; the crater was now cleared up except of enemy dead, whose partly buried arms and legs still stuck out here and there. A company of the Third Foreign Legion had just come into the crater and had taken station at the loopholes under the parapet of sandbags.

As soon as the telephone wires were stretched as far as our crater a message came for me to remain where I was until further orders. I had just received this message and was walking along, slowly, behind the rank of soldiers, who stood leaning against the parapet with their rifles thrust through the loops, when somebody said in English—in East Side New York English I mean—"Ah, there, Doc!"

A soldier had turned toward me, both hands still grasping his resting rifle. In the "horizon blue" uniform and ugly, iron, shrapnel-proof helmet strapped to his bullet head I failed to recognize him.

"It's me, 'Duck' Werner," he said, as I stood hesitating. . . . You know who he is, political leader in the 50th Ward, here. I was astounded.

"What do you know about it?" he added. "Me in a tin derby potting Fritzies! And there's Heinie, too, and Pick-em-up Joe—the whole bunch sewed up in this here trench, oh my God!"

I went over to him and stood leaning against the parapet beside him.

"Duck," I said, amazed, "how did *you* come to enlist in the Foreign Legion?"

"Aw," he replied with infinite disgust, "I got drunk."

"Where?"

"Me and Heinie and Joe was follerin' the races down to Boolong when this here war come and put everything on the blink. Aw, hell, sez I, come on back to Parus an' look 'em over before we skiddoo home—meanin' the dames an' all like that. Say, we done what I said; we come back to Parus, an' we got in wrong! Listen, Doc; them dames had went crazy over this here war graft. Veeve France, sez they. An' by God! we veeved.

"An' one of 'em at Maxeems got me soused, and others they fixed up Heinie an' Joe, an' we was all wavin' little American flags and yellin' 'To hell with the Hun!' Then there was a interval for which I can't account to nobody.

"All I seem to remember is my marchin' in the boolyvard along with a guy in baggy red pants, and my chewin' the rag in a big, hot room full o' soldiers; an' Heinie an' Joe they was shoutin', 'Wow! Lemme at 'em. Veeve la France!' Wha' d'ye know about me? Ain't I the mark from home?"

"You didn't realize that you were enlisting?"

"Aw, does it make any difference to these here guys what you reelize, or what you don't? I ask you, Doc?"

He spat disgustedly upon the sand, rolled his quid into the other cheek, wiped his thin lips with the back of his right hand, then his fingers mechanically sought the trigger guard again and he cast a perfunctory squint up at the parapet.

"Believe me," he said, "a guy can veeve himself into any kind of trouble if he yells loud enough. I'm getting mine."

"Well, Duck," I said, "it's a good game———"

"Aw," he retorted angrily, "it ain't my graft an' you know it. What do I care who veeves over here?—An' the 50th Ward goin' to hell an' all!"

I strove to readjust my mind to understand what he had said. I was, you know, that year, the Citizen's Anti-Graft leader in the 50th Ward. . . . I am, still, if I live; and if I ever can get anything into my head except the stupendous din of this war and the cataclysmic problems depending upon its outcome. . . . Well, it was odd to remember that petty political conflict as I stood there in the trenches under the gigantic shadow of world-wide disaster—to find myself there, talking with this sallow, wiry, shifty ward leader—this corrupt little local tyrant whom I had opposed in the 50th Ward—this ex-lightweight bruiser, ex-gunman—this dirty little political procurer who had been and was everything brutal, stealthy, and corrupt.

I looked at him curiously; turned and glanced along the line where, presently, I recognized his two familiars, Heinie Baum and Pick-em-up Joe Brady with whom he had started off to "Parus" on a month's summer junket, and with whom he had stumbled so ludicrously into the riff-raff ranks of the 3rd Foreign Legion. Doubtless the 1st and 2nd Legions couldn't stand him and his two friends, although in one company there were many Americans serving.

Thinking of these things, the thunder of the cannonade shaking sand from the parapet, I became conscious that the rat eyes of Duck Werner were furtively watching me.

"You can do me dirt, now, can't you, Doc?" he said with a leer.

"How do you mean?"

"Aw, as if I had to tell you. I got some sense left."

Suddenly his sallow visage under the iron helmet became distorted with helpless fury; he fairly snarled; his thin lips writhed as he spat out the suspicion which had seized him:

"By God, Doc, if you do that!—if you leave me here caged up an' go home an' raise hell in the 50th—with me an' Joe here——"

After a breathless pause: "Well," said I, "what will you do about it?"—for he was looking murder at me.

Neither of us spoke again for a few moments; an officer, smoking a cigarette, came up between Heinie and Pick-em-up Joe, adjusted a periscope and set his eye to it. Through the sky above us the shells raced as though hundreds of shaky express trains were rushing overhead on rickety aërial tracks, deafening the world with their outrageous clatter.

"Listen, Doc——"

I looked up into his altered face—a sallow, earnest face, fiercely intent. Every atom of the man's intelligence was alert, concentrated on me, on my expression, on my slightest movement.

"Doc," he said, "let's talk business. We're men, we are, you an' me. I've fought you plenty times. I *know*. An' I guess you are on to me, too. I ain't no squealer; you know that anyway. Perhaps I'm everything else

141

you claim I am when you make parlor speeches to Gussie an' Reggie an' when you stand on a bar'l in Avenoo A an' say: 'my friends' to Billy an' Izzy an' Pete the Wop.

"All right. Go to it! I'm it. I got mine. That's what I'm there for. But—when I get mine, the guys that back me get theirs, too. My God, Doc, let's talk business! What's a little graft between friends?"

"Duck," I said, "you own the 50th Ward. You are no fool. Why is it not possible for you to understand that some men don't graft?"

"Aw, can it!" he retorted fiercely. "What else is there to chase except graft? What else is there, I ask you? Graft! Ain't there graft into everything God ever made? An' don't the smart guy get it an' take his an' divide the rest same as you an' me?"

"You can't comprehend that I don't graft, can you, Duck?"

"What do you call it what you get, then? The wages of Reeform? And what do you hand out to your lootenants an' your friends?"

"Service."

"Hey? Well, all right. But what's in it for you? Where do you get yours, Doc?"

"There's nothing in it for me except to give honest service to the people who trust me."

"Listen," he persisted with a sort of ferocious patience; "you ain't on no bar'l now; an' you ain't calling no Ginneys and no Kikes your friends. You're just talkin' to me like there wasn't nobody else onto this damn planet excep' us two guys. Get that?"

"I do."

"And I'm tellin' you that I get mine same as any one who ain't a loonatic. Get that?"

"Certainly."

"All right. Now I know you ain't no nut. Which means that you get yours, whatever you call it. And *now* will you talk business?"

"What business do you want to talk, Duck?" I added; "I should say that you already have your hands rather full of business and Lebel rifles——"

"Aw' Gawd; *this?* This ain't business. I was a damn fool and I'm doin' time like any souse what the bulls pinch. Only I get more than thirty days, I do. That's what's killin' me,

Doc!—Duck Werner in a tin lid, suckin' soup an' shootin' Fritzies when I oughter be in Noo York with me fren's lookin' after business. Can you beat it?" he ended fiercely.

He chewed hard on his quid for a few moments, staring blankly into space with the detached ferocity of a caged tiger.

"What are they a-doin' over there in the 50th?" he demanded. "How do I know whose knifin' me with the boys? I don't mean your party. You're here same as I am. I mean Mike the Kike, and the regular Reepublican nomination, I do. . . . And, how do I know when *you* are going back?"

I was silent.

"*Are* you?"

"Perhaps."

"Doc, will you talk business, man to man?"

"Duck, to tell you the truth, the hell that is in full blast over here—this gigantic, worldwide battle of nations—leaves me, for the time, uninterested in ward politics."

"Stop your kiddin'."

"Can't you comprehend it?"

"Aw, what do you care about what Kink wins?

If we was Kinks, you an' me, all right. But we ain't Doc. We're little fellows. Our graft ain't big like the Dutch Emperor's, but maybe it comes just as regular on pay day. Ich ka bibble."

"Duck," I said, "you explain your presence here by telling me that you enlisted while drunk. How do you explain my being here?"

"You're a Doc. I guess there must be big money into it," he returned with a wink.

"I draw no pay."

"I believe you," he remarked, leering. "Say, don't you do that to me, Doc. I may be unfortunit; I'm a poor damn fool an' I know it. But don't tell me you're here for your health."

"I won't repeat it, Duck," I said, smiling.

"Much obliged. Now for God's sake let's talk business. You think you've got me cinched. You think you can go home an' raise hell in the 50th while I'm doin' time into these here trenches. You sez to yourself, 'O there ain't nothin' to it!' An' then you tickles yourself under the ribs, Doc. You better make a deal with me, do you hear? Gimme mine, and you can have yours, too; and between us, if we

145

work together, we can hand one to Mike the Kike that'll start every ambulance in the city after him. Get me?"

"There's no use discussing such things——"

"All right. I won't ask you to make it fifty-fifty. Gimme half what I oughter have. You can fix it with Curley Tim Brady——"

"Duck, this is no time——"

"Hell! It's all the time I've got! What do you expec' out here, a caffy dansong? I don't see no corner gin-mills around neither. Listen, Doc, quit up-stagin'! You an' me kick the block off'n this here Kike-Wop if we get together. All I ask of you is to talk business——"

I moved aside, and backward a little way, disgusted with the ratty soul of the man, and stood looking at the soldiers who were digging out bombproof burrows all along the trench and shoring up the holes with heavy, green planks.

Everybody was methodically busy in one way or another behind the long rank of Legionaries who stood at the loops, the butts of the Lebel rifles against their shoulders.

Some sawed planks to shore up dugouts; some were constructing short ladders out of the trunks of slender green saplings; some filled sacks with earth to fill the gaps on the parapet above; others sharpened pegs and drove them into the dirt façade of the trench, one above the other, as footholds for the men when a charge was ordered.

Behind me, above my head, wild flowers and long wild grasses drooped over the raw edge of the parados, and a few stalks of ripening wheat trailed there or stood out against the sky—an opaque, uncertain sky which had been so calmly blue, but which was now sickening with that whitish pallor which presages a storm.

Once or twice there came the smashing tinkle of glass as a periscope was struck and a vexed officer, still holding it, passed it to a rifleman to be laid aside.

Only one man was hit. He had been fitting a shutter to the tiny embrasure between sandbags where a machine gun was to be mounted; and the bullet came through and entered his head in the center of the triangle between nose and eyebrows.

A little later when I was returning from that job, walking slowly along the trench, Pick-em-up Joe hailed me cheerfully, and I glanced up to where he and Heinie stood with their rifles thrust between the sandbags and their grimy fists clutching barrel and butt.

"Hello, Heinie!" I said pleasantly. "How are you, Joe?"

"Commong ça va?" inquired Heinie, evidently mortified at his situation and condition, but putting on the careless front of a gunman in a strange ward.

Pick-em-up Joe added jauntily: "Well, Doc, what's the good word?"

"France," I replied, smiling; "Do you know a better word?"

"Yes," he said, "Noo York. Say, what's your little graft over here, Doc?"

"You and I reverse rôles, Pick-em-up; you *stop* bullets; *I* pick 'em up — after you're through with 'em."

"The hell you say!" he retorted, grinning.

"Well, grab it from me, if it wasn't for the Jack Johnsons and the gas, a gun fight in the old 50th would make this war look like Luna Park! It listens like it, too, only this here show is all fi-*nally*, with Bingle's Band playin' circus tunes an' the supes hollerin' like they seen real money."

He was a merry ruffian, and he controlled the "coke" graft in the 50th while Heinie was perpetual bondsman for local Magdalenes.

"Well, ain't we in Dutch—us three guys!" he remarked with forced carelessness. "We sure done it that time."

"Did you do business with Duck?" inquired Pick-em-up, curiously.

"Not so he noticed it. Joe, can't you and Heinie rise to your opportunities? This is the first time in your lives you've ever been decent, ever done a respectable thing. Can't you start in and live straight—think straight? You're wearing the uniform of God's own soldiers; you're standing shoulder to shoulder with men who are fighting God's own battle. The fate of every woman, every child, every unborn baby in Europe—and in America, too—depends on your bravery. If you don't win out, it will be our turn next. If you don't stop the Huns—if you don't come back at them and wipe them out, the world will not be worth inhabiting."

I stepped nearer: "Heinie," I said, "you know what your trade has been, and what it is called. Here's your chance to clean yourself. Joe—you've dealt out misery, insanity, death, to women and children. You're called the Coke King of the East Side. Joe, we'll get you sooner or later. Don't take the trouble to doubt it. Why not order a new pack and a fresh deal? Why not resolve to live straight from this moment—here where you have taken your place in the ranks among real men—here where this army stands for liberty, for the right to live! You've got your chance to become a real man; so has Heinie. And when you come back, we'll stand by you——"

"An' gimme a job choppin' tickets in the subway!" snarled Heinie. "Expec' me to squeal f'r that? Reeform, hey? Show me a livin' in it an' I carry a banner. But there ain't nothing into it. How's a guy to live if there ain't no graft into nothin'?"

Joe touched his gas-mask with a sneer: "He's pushin' the yellow stuff at us, Heinie," he said; and to me: "You get *yours* all right. I don't know what it is, but you get it, same as me an' Heinie an' Duck. *I* don't know what it is," he repeated impatiently; "maybe it's dough; maybe it's them suffragettes with their silk feet an' white gloves what clap their hands at you. *I* ain't saying nothin' to *you*, am I? Then lemme alone an' go an' talk business with Duck over there——"

Officers passed rapidly between the speaker and me and continued east and west along the ranks of riflemen, repeating in calm, steady voices:

"Fix bayonets, *mes enfants;* make as little noise as possible. Everybody ready in ten minutes. Ladders will be distributed. Take them with you. The bomb-throwers will leave the trench first. Put on goggles and respirators. Fix bayonets and set one foot on the pegs and ladders . . . all ready in seven minutes. Three mines will be exploded. Take

and hold the craters. . . . Five minutes! . . .
When the mines explode that is your signal.
Bombers lead. Give them a leg up and fol-
low. . . . Three minutes. . . ."

From a communication trench a long file of
masked bomb-throwers appeared, loaded sacks
slung under their left arms, bombs clutched
in their right hands; and took stations at
every ladder and row of freshly driven pegs.

"One minute!" repeated the officers, select-
ing their own ladders and drawing their long
knives and automatics.

As I finished adjusting my respirator and
goggles a muffled voice at my elbow began:
"Be a sport, Doc! Gimme a chanst! Make
it fifty-fifty——"

"*Allez!*" shouted an officer through his respirator.

Against the sky all along the parapet's edge
hundreds of bayonets wavered for a second;
then dark figures leaped up, scrambled,
crawled forward, rose, ran out into the sun-
less, pallid light.

Like surf bursting along a coast a curtain
of exploding shells stretched straight across the

débris of what had been a meadow—a long line of livid obscurity split with flame and storms of driving sand and gravel. Shrapnel leisurely unfolded its cottony coils overhead and the iron helmets rang under the hail.

Men fell forward, backward, sideways, remaining motionless, or rolling about, or rising to limp on again. There was smoke, now, and mire, and the unbroken rattle of machine guns.

Ahead, men were fishing in their sacks and throwing bombs like a pack of boys stoning a snake; I caught glimpses of them furiously at work from where I knelt beside one fallen man after another, desperately busy with my own business.

Bearers ran out where I was at work, not my own company but some French ambulance sections who served me as well as their own surgeons where, in a shell crater partly full of water, we found some shelter for the wounded.

Over us black smoke from the Jack Johnsons rolled as it rolls out of the stacks of soft-coal burning locomotives; the outrageous din never slackened, but our deafened ears had become insensible under the repeated blows of sound, yet not paralyzed. For I remember, squatting there in that shell crater, hearing a cricket tranquilly tuning up between the thunderclaps which shook earth and sods down on us and wrinkled the pool of water at our feet.

The Legion had taken the trench; but the place was a rabbit warren where hundreds of holes and burrows and ditches and communicating runways made a bewildering maze.

And everywhere in the dull, flame-shot obscurity, the Legionaries ran about like ghouls in their hoods and round, hollow eye-holes; masked faces, indistinct in the smoke, loomed grotesque and horrible as Ku-Klux where the bayonets were at work digging out the enemy from blind burrows, turning them up from their bloody forms.

Rifles blazed down into bomb-proofs, cracked steadily over the heads of comrades who piled up sandbags to block communication trenches; grenade-bombs rained down through the smoke into trenches, blowing bloody gaps in huddling masses of struggling Teutons until they flattened back against the parados and lifted arms and gun-butts stammering out, "Comrades! Comrades!"—in the ghastly irony of surrender.

A man whose entire helmet, gas-mask, and face had been blown off, and who was still alive and trying to speak, stiffened, relaxed, and died in my arms. As I rolled him aside and turned to the next man whom the bearers were lowering into the crater, his respirator and goggles fell apart, and I found myself looking into the ashy face of Duck Werner.

As we laid him out and stripped away iron helmet and tunic, he said in a natural and distinct voice.

"Through the belly, Doc. Gimme a drink."

There was no more water or stimulant at the moment and the puddle in the crater was bloody. He said, patiently, "All right; I can wait. . . . It's in the belly. . . . It ain't nothin', is it?"

I said something reassuring, something about the percentage of recovery I believe, for I was exceedingly busy with Duck's anatomy.

"Pull me through, Doc?" he inquired calmly.

"Sure. . . ."

"Aw, listen, Doc. Don't hand me no cones of hokey-pokey. Gimme a deck of the stuff. Dope out the coke. Do I get mine this trip?"

I looked at him, hesitating.

"Listen, Doc, am I hurted bad? Gimme a hones' deal. Do I croak?"

"Don't talk, Duck——"

"Dope it straight. *Do* I?"

"Yes."

"I thought you'd say that," he returned serenely. "Now I'm goin' to fool you, same as I fooled them guys at Bellevue the night that Mike the Kike shot me up in the subway."

A pallid sneer stretched his thin and burning lips; in his ratty eyes triumph gleamed.

"I've went through worse than this. I ain't hurted bad. I ain't got mine just yet, old scout! Would I leave meself croak—an' that bum, Mike the Kike, handin' me fren's the ha-ha! Gawd," he muttered hazily, as though his mind was beginning to cloud, "just f'r that I'll get up an'—an' go—home—" His voice flattened out and he lay silent.

Working over the next man beyond him and glancing around now and then to discover a *brancardier* who might take Duck to the rear, I presently caught his eyes fixed on me.

"Say, Doc, will you talk—business?" he asked in a dull voice.

"Be quiet, Duck, the bearers will be here in a minute or two——"

"T'hell wit them guys! I'm askin' you will you make it fifty-fifty—'r' somethin'—" Again his voice trailed away, but his bright ratty eyes were indomitable.

I was bloodily occupied with another patient when something struck me on the shoulder—a human hand, clutching it. Duck was sitting upright, eyes a-glitter, the other hand pressed heavily over his abdomen.

"Fifty-fifty!" he cried in a shrill voice. "F'r Christ's sake, Doc, talk business—" And life went out inside him—like the flame of a suddenly snuffed candle—while he still sat there. . . .

I heard the air escaping from his lungs

before he toppled over. . . . I swear to you it sounded like a whispered word—"business."

"Then came their gas—a great, thick, yellow billow of it pouring into our shell hole. . . . I couldn't get my mask on fast enough . . . and here I am, Gray, wondering, but really knowing. . . . Are you stopping at the Club tonight?"

"Yes."

Vail got to his feet unsteadily: "I'm feeling rather done in. . . . Won't sit up any longer, I guess. . . . See you in the morning?"

"Yes," said Gray.

"Good-night, then. Look in on me if you leave before I'm up."

And that is how Gray saw him before he sailed—stopped at his door, knocked, and, receiving no response, opened and looked in. After a few moments' silence he understood that the "Seed of Death" had sprouted.

CHAPTER XIII

MULETEERS

Lying far to the southwest of the battle line, only when a strong northwest wind blew could Sainte Lesse hear the thudding of cannon beyond the horizon. And once, when the northeast wind had blown steadily for a week, on the wings of the driving drizzle had come a faint but dreadful odour which hung among the streets and lanes until the wind changed.

Except for the carillon, nothing louder than the call of a cuckoo, the lowing of cattle or a goatherd's piping ever broke the summer silence in the little town. Birds sang; a shallow river rippled; breezes ruffled green grain into long, silvery waves across the valley; sunshine fell on quiet streets, on scented gardens unsoiled by war, on groves and meadows, and on the stone-edged brink of brimming pools where washerwomen knelt among the wild flowers, splashing amid floating pyramids of snowy suds.

And into the exquisite peace of this little paradise rode John Burley with a thousand American mules.

The town had been warned of this impending visitation; had watched preparations for it during April and May when a corral was erected down in a meadow and some huts and stables were put up among the groves of poplar and sycamore, and a small barracks was built to accommodate the negro guardians of the mules and a peloton of gendarmes under a fat brigadier.

Sainte Lesse as yet knew nothing personally of the American mule or of Burley. Saine Lesse heard both before it beheld either —Burley's loud, careless, swaggering voice above the hee-haw of his trampling herds:

"All I ask for is human food, Smith—not luxuries—just food!—and that of the commonest kind."

And now an immense volume of noise and

dust enveloped the main street of Sainte Lesse, stilling the quiet noon gossip of the town, silencing the birds, awing the town dogs so that their impending barking died to amazed gurgles drowned in the din of the mules.

Astride a cream-coloured, wall-eyed mule, erect in his saddle, talkative, gesticulating, good-humoured, famished but gay, rode Burley at the head of the column, his reckless grey eyes glancing amiably right and left at the good people of Sainte Lesse who clustered silently at their doorways under the trees to observe the passing of this noisy, unfamiliar procession.

Mules, dust; mules, dust, and then more mules, all enveloped in dust, clattering, ambling, trotting, bucking, shying, kicking, halting, backing; and here and there an American negro cracking a long snake whip with strange, aboriginal ejaculations; and three white men in khaki riding beside the trampling column, smoking cigarettes.

"Sticky" Smith and "Kid" Glenn rode mules on the column's flank; Burley continued to lead on his wall-eyed animal, preceded now by the fat brigadier of the gendarmerie, upon whom he had bestowed a cigarette.

Burley, talking all the while from his saddle to whoever cared to listen, or to himself if nobody cared to listen, rode on in the van under the ancient bell-tower of Sainte Lesse, where a slim, dark-eyed girl looked up at him as he passed, a faint smile hovering on her lips.

"Bong jour, Mademoiselle," continued Burley, saluting her *en passant* with two fingers at the vizor of his khaki cap, as he had seen British officers salute. "I compliment you on your silent but eloquent welcome to me, my comrades, my coons, and my mules. Your charming though slightly melancholy smile bids us indeed welcome to your fair city. I thank you; I thank all the inhabitants for this unprecedented ovation. Doubtless a municipal banquet awaits us——"

Sticky Smith spurred up.

"Did you see the inn?" he asked. "There it is, to the right."

"It looks good to me," said Burley.

"Everything looks good to me except these accursed mules. Thank God, that seems to be the corral—down in the meadow there, Brigadeer!"

The fat brigadier drew bridle; Burley burst into French:

"Esker—esker——"

"*Oui*," nodded the brigadier, "that is where we are going."

"Bong!" exclaimed Burley with satisfaction; and, turning to Sticky Smith: "Stick, tell the coons to hustle. We're there!"

Then, above the trampling, whip-cracking, and shouting of the negroes, from somewhere high in the blue sky overhead, out of limpid, cloudless heights floated a single bell-note, then another, another, others exquisitely sweet and clear, melting into a fragment of heavenly melody.

Burley looked up into the sky; the negroes raised their sweating, dark faces in pleased astonishment; Stick and Kid Glenn lifted puzzled visages to the zenith. The fat brigadier smiled and waved his cigarette:

"*Il est midi, messieurs.* That is the carillon of Sainte Lesse."

The angelic melody died away. Then, high in the old bell-tower, a great resonant bell struck twelve times.

Said the brigadier:

"When the wind is right, they can hear our big bell, Bayard, out there in the first line trenches——"

Again he waved his cigarette toward the northeast, then reined in his horse and backed off into the flowering meadow, while the first of the American mules entered the corral, the herd following pellmell.

The American negroes went with the mules to a hut prepared for them inside the corral —it having been previously and carefully explained to France that an American mule without its negro complement was as galvanic and unaccountable as a beheaded chicken.

Burley burst into French again, like a shrapnel shell:

"Esker—esker——"

"*Oui*," said the fat brigadier, "there is an excellent inn up the street, messieurs." And he saluted their uniform, the same being constructed of cotton khaki, with a horseshoe on the arm and an oxidized metal mule on the collar. The brigadier wondered at and admired the minute nicety of administrative detail characterizing a government which clothed even its muleteers so becomingly, yet with such modesty and dignity.

He could not know that the uniform was unauthorized and the insignia an invention of Sticky Smith, aiming to counteract any social stigma that might blight his sojourn in France.

"For," said Sticky Smith, before they went aboard the transport at New Orleans, "if you dress a man in khaki, with some gimcrack on his sleeve and collar, you're level with anybody in Europe. Which," he added to Burley, "will make it pleasant if any emperors or kings drop in on us for a drink or a quiet game behind the lines."

"Also," added Burley, "it goes with the ladies." And he and Kid Glenn purchased uniforms similar to Smith's and had the horseshoe and mule fastened to sleeve and collar.

"They'll hang you fellows for francs-tireurs," remarked a battered soldier of fortune from the wharf as the transport cast off and glided gradually away from the sun-blistered docks.

"Hang *who?*" demanded Burley loudly from the rail above.

"What's a frank-tiroor?" inquired Sticky Smith.

"And who'll hang us?" shouted Kid Glenn from the deck of the moving steamer.

"The Germans will if they catch you in that uniform," retorted the battered soldier of fortune derisively. "You chorus-boy mule drivers will wish you wore overalls and one suspender if the Dutch Kaiser nails you!"

CHAPTER XIV.

They had been nearly three weeks on the voyage, three days in port, four more on cattle trains, and had been marching since morning from the nearest railway station at Estville-sur-Lesse.

Now, lugging their large leather hold-alls, they started up the main street of Sainte Lesse, three sunburnt, loud-talking Americans, young, sturdy, careless of glance and voice and gesture, perfectly self-satisfied.

Their footsteps echoed loudly on the pavement of this still, old town, lying so quietly in the shadow of its aged trees and its sixteenth century belfry, where the great bell, Bayard, had hung for hundreds of years, and, tier on tier above it, clustered in set ranks the fixed bells of the ancient carillon.

167

"Some skyscraper," observed Burley, patronizing the bell-tower with a glance.

As he spoke, they came to the inn, a very ancient hostelry built into a remnant of the old town wall, and now a part of it. On the signboard was painted a white doe; and that was the name of the inn.

So they trooped through the stone-arched tunnel, ushered by a lame innkeeper; and Burley, chancing to turn his head and glance back through the shadowy stone passage, caught a glimpse in the outer sunshine of the girl whose dark eyes had inspired him with jocular eloquence as he rode on his mule under the bell-tower of Sainte Lesse.

"A peach," he said to Smith. And the sight of her apparently going to his head, he burst into French: "Tray chick! Tray, tray chick! I'm glad I've got on this uniform and not overalls and one suspender."

"What's biting you?" inquired Smith.

"Nothing, Stick, nothing. But I believe I've seen the prettiest girl in the world right here in this two-by-four town."

Stick glanced over his shoulder, then shrugged:

"She's ornamental, only she's got a sad on."

But Burley trudged on with his leather hold-all, muttering to himself something about the prettiest girl in the world.

The "prettiest girl in the world" continued her way unconscious of the encomiums of John Burley and the critique of Sticky Smith. Her way, however, seemed to be the way of Burley and his two companions, for she crossed the sunny street and entered the White Doe by the arched door and tunnel-like passage.

Unlike them, however, she turned to the right in the stone corridor, opened a low wooden door, crossed the inn parlour, ascended a short stairway, and entered a bedroom.

Here, standing before a mirror, she unpinned her straw hat, smoothed her dark hair, resting her eyes pensively for a few moments on her reflected face. Then she sauntered listlessly about the little room in performance of those trivial, aimless offices, entirely feminine, such as opening all the drawers in her clothes-press, smoothing out various frilly objects and fabrics, investigating a little gilded box and thoughtfully inspecting its contents, which consisted of hairpins. Fussing here, lingering there, loitering by her bird-cage, where a canary cheeped its greeting and hopped and hopped; bending over a cluster of white phlox in a glass of water to inhale the old-fashioned perfume, she finally tied on a fresh apron and walked slowly out to the ancient, vaulted kitchen.

An old peasant woman was cooking, while a young one washed dishes.

"Are the American gentlemen still at table, Julie?" she inquired.

"Mademoiselle Maryette, they are devouring everything in the house!" exclaimed old Julie, flinging both hands toward heaven. "*Tenez*, mamzelle, I have heard of eating in ancient days, I have read of Gargantua, I have been told of banquets, of feasting, of appetites! But there is one American in there! Mamzelle Maryette, if I should swear to you that he is on his third chicken and that a row of six pint bottles of '93 Margaux stand empty on the cloth at his elbow, I should do no penance for untruthfulness. *Tenez, Mamzelle Maryette, regardez un peu par l'oubliette—*" And old Julie slid open the wooden shutter on the crack and Maryette bent forward and surveyed the dining room outside.

They were laughing very loud in there, these three Americans—three powerful, sunscorched young men, very much at their ease around the table, draining the red Bordeaux by goblets, plying knife and fork with joyous and undiminished vigour.

The tall one with the crisp hair and clear, grayish eyes—he of the three chickens—was already achieving the third—a crisply browned bird, fresh from the spit, fragrant and smoking hot. At intervals he buttered great slices of rye bread, or disposed of an entire young potato, washing it down with a goblet of red wine, but always he returned to the rich roasted fowl which he held, still impaled upon its spit, and which he carved as he ate, wings, legs, breast falling in steaming flakes under his skillful knife blade.

Sticky Smith finally pushed aside his drained glass and surveyed an empty plate frankly and regretfully, unable to continue. He said:

"I'm going to bed and I'm going to sleep twenty-four hours. After that I'm going to eat for twenty-four more hours, and then I'll be in good shape. Bong soir."

"Aw, stick around with the push!" remonstrated Kid Glenn thickly, impaling another potato upon his fork and gesticulating with it.

Smith gazed with surfeited but hopeless envy upon Burley's magnificent work with knife and fork, saw him crack a seventh bottle of Bordeaux, watched him empty the first goblet.

But even Glenn's eyes began to dull in spite of himself, his head nodded mechanically at every mouthful achieved.

"I gotta call it off, Jack," he yawned. "Stick and I need the sleep if you don't. So here's where we quit——"

"Let me tell you about that girl," began Burley. "I never saw a prettier—" But

Glenn had appetite neither for food nor romance:

"Say, listen. Have a heart, Jack! We need the sleep!"

Stick had already risen; Glenn shoved back his chair with a gigantic yawn and shambled to his feet.

"I want to tell you," insisted Burley, "that she's what the French call tray, tray chick——"

Stick pointed furiously at the fowl:

"Chick? I'm fed up on chick! Maybe she is some chick, as you say, but it doesn't interest me. Goo'bye. Don't come battering at my door and wake me up, Jack. Be a sport and lemme alone——"

He turned and shuffled out, and Glenn followed, his Mexican spurs clanking.

Burley jeered them:

"Mollycoddles! Come on and take in the town with us!"

But they slammed the door behind them, and he heard them stumbling and clanking up stairs.

So Burley, gazing gravely at his empty

plate, presently emptied the last visible bottle of Bordeaux, then stretching his mighty arms and superb chest, fished out a cigarette, set fire to it, unhooked the cartridge-belt and holster from the back of his chair, buckled it on, rose, pulled on his leather-peaked cap, and drew a deep breath of contentment.

For a moment he stood in the centre of the room, as though in pleasant meditation, then he slowly strode toward the street door, murmuring to himself: "Tray, tray chick. The prettiest girl in the world. . . . La ploo belle fille du monde . . . la ploo belle. . . ."

He strolled as far as the corral down in the meadow by the stream, where he found the negro muleteers asleep and the mules already watered and fed.

For a while he hobnobbed with the three gendarmes on duty there, practicing his kind of French on them and managing to understand and be understood more or less—probably less.

But the young man was persistent; he desired to become that easy master of the French language that his tongue-tied comrades believed him to be. So he practiced garrulously upon the polite, suffering gendarmes.

He related to them his experience on shipboard with a thousand mutinous mules to pacify, feed, water, and otherwise cherish. They had, it appeared, encountered no submarines, but enjoyed several alarms from destroyers which eventually proved to be British.

"A cousin of mine," explained Burley, "Ned Winters, of El Paso, went down on the steamer *John B. Doty*, with eleven hundred mules and six niggers. The Boches torpedoed the ship and then raked the boats. I'd like to get a crack at one Boche before I go back to God's country."

The gendarmes politely but regretfully agreed that it was impracticable for Burley to get a crack at a Hun; and the American presently took himself off to the corral, after distributing cigarettes and establishing cordial relations with the Sainte Lesse Gendarmerie.

He waked up a negro and inspected the

mules; that took a long time. Then he sought out the negro blacksmith, awoke him, and wrote out some directions.

"The idea is," he explained, "that whenever the French in this sector need mules they draw on our corral. We are supposed to keep ten or eleven hundred mules here all the time and look after them. Shipments come every two weeks, I believe. So after you've had another good nap, George, you wake up your boys and get busy. And there'll be trouble if things are not in running order by tomorrow night."

"Yas, suh, Mistuh Burley," nodded the sleepy blacksmith, still blinking in the afternoon sunshine.

"And if you need an interpreter," added Burley, "always call on me until you learn French enough to get on. Understand, George?"

"Yas, suh."

"Because," said Burley, walking away, "a thorough knowledge of French idioms is necessary to prevent mistakes. When in doubt always apply to me, George, for only a master of the language is competent to deal with these French people."

It was his one vanity, his one weakness. Perhaps, because he so ardently desired proficiency, he had already deluded himself with the belief that he was a master of French.

So, belt and loaded holster sagging, and large silver spurs clicking and clinking at every step, John Burley sauntered back along the almost deserted street of Sainte Lesse, thinking sometimes of his mules, sometimes of the French language, and every now and then of a dark-eyed, dark-haired girl whose delicately flushed and pensive gaze he had encountered as he had ridden into Sainte Lesse under the old belfry.

"Stick Smith's a fool," he thought to himself impatiently. "Tray chick doesn't mean 'some chicken.' It means a pretty girl, in French."

He looked up at the belfry as he passed under it, and at the same moment, from beneath the high, gilded dragon which crowned its topmost spire, a sweet bell-note floated, another, others succeeding in crystalline

177

sweetness, linked in a fragment of some ancient melody. Then they ceased; then came a brief silence; the great bell he had heard before struck five times.

"Lord!—that's pretty," he murmured, moving on and turning into the arched tunnel which was the entrance to the White Doe Inn.

Wandering at random, he encountered the innkeeper in the parlour, studying a crumpled newspaper through horn-rimmed spectacles on his nose.

"Tray jolie," said Burley affably, seating himself with an idea of further practice in French.

"*Plait-il?*"

"The bells—tray beau!"

The old man straightened his bent shoulders a little proudly.

"For thirty years, m'sieu, I have been Carillonneur of Sainte Lesse." He smiled; then, saddened, he held out both hands toward Burley. The fingers were stiff and crippled with rheumatism.

"No more," he said slowly; "the carillon is

178

ended for me. The great art is no more for Jean Courtray, Master of Bells."

"What is a carillon?" inquired John Burley simply.

Blank incredulity was succeeded by a shocked expression on the old man's visage. After a silence, in mild and patient protest, he said:

"I am Jean Courtray, Carillonneur of Sainte Lesse. . . . Have you never heard of the carillon of Sainte Lesse, or of me?"

"Never," said Burley. "We don't have anything like that in America."

The old carillonneur, Jean Courtray, began to speak in a low voice of his art, his profession, and of the great carillon of forty-six bells in the ancient tower of Sainte Lesse.

A carillon, he explained, is a company of fixed bells tuned according to the chromatic scale and ranging through several octaves. These bells, rising tier above tier in a belfry, the smallest highest, the great, ponderous bells of the bass notes lowest, are not free to swing, but are fixed to huge beams, and are sounded by clappers connected by a wilderness of wires to a keyboard which is played upon by the bell-master or carillonneur.

He explained that the office of bell-master was an ancient one and greatly honoured; that the bell-master was also a member of the municipal government; that his salary was a fixed one; that not only did he play upon the carillon on fête days, market days, and particular occasions, but he also travelled and gave concerts upon the few existing carillons of other ancient towns and cities, not alone in France where carillons were few, but in Belgium and Holland, where they still were comparatively many, although the German barbarians had destroyed some of the best at Liége, Arras, Dixmude, Termonde, and Ypres.

"Monsieur," he went on in a voice which began to grow a little unsteady, "the Huns have destroyed the ancient carillons of Louvain and of Mechlin. In the superb belltower of Saint Rombold I have played for a thousand people; and the Carillonneur, Monsieur Vincent, and the great bell-master, Josef Denyn, have come to me to congratulate me with tears in their eyes—in their eyes——"

There were tears in his own now, and he bent his white head and looked down at the worn floor under his crippled feet.

"Alas," he said, "for Denyn—and for Saint Rombold's tower. The Hun has passed that way."

After a silence:

"Who is it now plays the carillon in Sainte Lesse?" asked Burley.

"My daughter, Maryette. Sainte Lesse has honoured me in my daughter, whom I myself instructed. My daughter—the little child of my old age, monsieur—is mistress of the bells of Sainte Lesse. . . . They call her Carillon-nette in Sainte Lesse——"

The door opened and the girl came in.

CHAPTER XV

Sticky Smith and Kid Glenn remained a week at Sainte Lesse, then left with the negroes for Calais to help bring up another cargo of mules, the arrival of which was daily expected.

A peloton of the Train-des-Equipages and three Remount troopers arrived at Sainte Lesse to take over the corral. John Burley remained to explain and interpret the American mule to these perplexed troopers.

Morning, noon, and night he went clanking down to the corral, his cartridge belt and holster swinging at his hip. But sometimes he had a little leisure.

Sainte Lesse knew him as a mighty eater and as a lusty drinker of good red wine; as a mighty and garrulous talker, too, he became known, ready to accost anybody in the quiet and subdued old town and explode into French at the slightest encouragement.

But Burley had only women and children and old men on whom to practice his earnest and voluble French, for everybody else was at the front.

Children adored him—adored his big, silver spurs, his cartridge belt and pistol, the metal mule decorating his tunic collar, his six feet two of height, his quick smile, the even white teeth and grayish eyes of this American muleteer, who always had a stick of barley sugar to give them or an amazing trick to perform for them with a handkerchief or coin that vanished under their very noses at the magic snap of his finger.

Old men gossiped willingly with him; women liked him and their rare smiles in the war-sobered town of Sainte Lesse were often for him as he sauntered along the quiet street, clanking, swaggering, affable, ready for conversation with anybody, and always ready for the small, confident hands that unceremoni-

183

ously clasped his when he passed by where children played.

As for Maryette Courtray, called Carillonnette, she mounted the bell-tower once every hour, from six in the morning until nine o'clock in the evening, to play the passing of Time toward that eternity into which it is always and ceaselessly moving.

After nine o'clock Carillonnette set the drum and wound it; and through the dark hours of the night the bells played mechanically every hour for a few moments before Bayard struck.

Between these duties the girl managed the old inn, to which, since the war, nobody came any more—and with these occupations her life was full—sufficiently full, perhaps, without the advent of John Burley.

They met with enough frequency for her, if not for him. Their encounters took place between her duties aloft at the keyboard under the successive tiers of bells and his intervals of prowling among his mules.

Sometimes he found her sewing in the parlour—she could have gone to her own room, of course; sometimes he encountered her in the corridor, in the street, in the walled garden behind the inn, where with basket and pan she gathered vegetables in season.

There was a stone seat out there, built against the southern wall, and in the shadowed coolness of it she sometimes shelled peas.

During such an hour of liberty from the bell-tower he found the dark-eyed little mistress of the bells sorting various vegetables and singing under her breath to herself the carillon music of Josef Denyn.

"Tray chick, mademoiselle," he said, with a cheerful self-assertion, to hide the embarrassment which always assailed him when he encountered her.

"You know, Monsieur Burley, you should not say '*très chic*' to me," she said, shaking her pretty head. "It sounds a little familiar and a little common."

"Oh," he exclaimed, very red. "I thought it was the thing to say."

She smiled, continuing to shell the peas, then, with her sensitive and slightly flushed face still lowered, she looked at him out of her dark blue eyes.

"Sometimes," she said, "young men say *'très chic.'* It depend on when and how one says it."

"Are there times when it is all right for me to say it?" he inquired.

"Yes, I think so. . . . How are your mules today?"

"The same," he said, "—ready to bite or kick or eat their heads off. The Remount took two hundred this morning."

"I saw them pass," said the girl. "I thought perhaps you also might be departing."

"Without coming to say good-bye—to *you!*" he stammered.

"Oh, conventions must be disregarded in time of war," she returned carelessly, continuing to shell peas. "I really thought I saw you riding away with the mules."

"That man," said Burley, much hurt, "was a bow-legged driver of the Train-des-Equipages. I don't think he resembles me."

As she made no comment and expressed no

186

contrition for her mistake, he gazed about him at the sunny garden with a depressed expression. However, this changed presently to a bright and hopeful one.

"Vooz ate tray, tray belle, mademoiselle!" he asserted cheerfully.

"Monsieur!" Vexed perhaps as much at her own quick blush as his abrupt eulogy, she bit her lip and looked at him with an ominously level gaze. Then, suddenly, she smiled.

"Monsieur Burley, one does *not* so express one's self without reason, without apropos, without—without encouragement——"

She blushed again, vividly. Under her wide straw hat her delicate, sensitive face and dark blue eyes were beautiful enough to inspire eulogy in any young man.

"Pardon," he said, confused by her reprimand and her loveliness. "I shall hereafter only *think* you are pretty, mademoiselle—mais je ne le dirais ploo."

"That would be perhaps more—*comme il faut*, monsieur."

"Ploo!" he repeated with emphasis. "Ploo jamais! Je vous jure——"

"*Merci;* it is not perhaps necessary to swear quite so solemnly, monsieur."

She raised her eyes from the pan, moving her small, sun-tanned hand through the heaps of green peas, filling her palm with them and idly letting them run through her slim fingers.

"L'amour," he said with an effort—"how funny it is—isn't it, mademoiselle?"

"I know nothing about it," she replied with decision, and rose with her pan of peas.

"Are you going, mademoiselle?"

"Yes."

"Have I offended you?"

"No."

He trailed after her down the garden path between rows of blue larkspurs and hollyhocks—just at her dainty heels, because the brick walk was too narrow for both of them.

"Ploo," he repeated appealingly.

Over her shoulder she said with disdain:

"It is not a topic for conversation among the young, monsieur—what you call *l'amour*." And she entered the kitchen, where he had not the effrontery to follow her.

That evening, toward sunset, returning

from the corral, he heard, high in the blue sky above him, her bell-music drifting; and involuntarily uncovering, he stood with bared head looking upward while the celestial melody lasted.

And that evening, too, being the fête of Alincourt, a tiny neighbouring village across the river, the bell-mistress went up into the tower after dinner and played for an hour for the little neighbour hamlet across the river Lesse.

All the people who remained in Sainte Lesse and in Alincourt brought out their chairs and their knitting in the calm, fragrant evening air and remained silent, sadly enraptured while the unseen player at her keyboard aloft in the belfry above set her carillon music adrift under the summer stars—golden harmonies that seemed born in the heavens from which they floated; clear, exquisitely sweet miracles of melody filling the world of darkness with magic messages of hope.

Those widowed or childless among her listeners for miles around in the darkness wept quiet tears, less bitter and less hopeless for the divine promise of the sky music which filled the night as subtly as the scent of flowers saturates the dusk.

Burley, listening down by the corral, leaned against a post, one powerful hand across his eyes, his cap clasped in the other, and in his heart the birth of things ineffable.

For an hour the carillon played. Then old Bayard struck ten times. And Burley thought of the trenches and wondered whether the mellow thunder of the great bell was audible out there that night.

CHAPTER XVI

DJACK

There came a day when he did not see Maryette as he left for the corral in the morning.

Her father, very stiff with rheumatism, sat in the sun outside the arched entrance to the inn.

"No," he said, "she is going to be gone all day today. She has set and wound the drum in the belfry so that the carillon shall play every hour while she is absent."

"Where has she gone?" inquired Burley.

"To play the carillon at Nivelle."

"Nivelle!" he exclaimed sharply.

"*Oui, monsieur.* The Mayor has asked for her. She is to play for an hour to entertain the wounded." He rested his withered cheek on his hand and looked out through the window at the sunshine with aged and tragic eyes. "It is very little to do for our wounded," he added aloud to himself.

Burley had sent twenty mules to Nivelle the night before, and had heard some disquieting rumours concerning that town.

Now he walked out past the dusky, arched passageway into the sunny street and continued northward under the trees to the barracks of the Gendarmerie.

"*Bon jour l'ami Gargantua!*" exclaimed the fat, jovial brigadier who had just emerged with boots shining, pipe-clay very apparent, and all rosy from a fresh shave.

"Bong joor, mon vieux copain!" replied Burley, preoccupied with some papers he was sorting. "Be good enough to look over my papers."

The brigadier took them and examined them.

"Are they *en règle?*" demanded Burley.

"*Parfaitement, mon ami.*"

"Will they take me as far as Nivelle?"

"Certainly. But your mules went forward last night with the Remount——"

"I know. I wish to inspect them again before the veterinary sees them. Telephone to the corral for a saddle mule."

The brigadier went inside to telephone and Burley started for the corral at the same time.

His cream-coloured, wall-eyed mule was saddled and waiting when he arrived; he stuffed his papers into the breast of his tunic and climbed into the saddle.

"Allongs!" he exclaimed. "Hoop!"

Half way to Nivelle, on an overgrown, bushy, circuitous path which was the only road open between Nivelle and Sainte Lesse, he overtook Maryette, driving her donkey and ancient market cart.

"Carillonnette!" he called out joyously. "Maryette! C'est je!"

The girl, astonished, turned her head, and he spurred forward on his wall-eyed mount, evincing cordial symptoms of pleasure in the encounter.

"Wee, wee!" he cried. "Je voolay veneer avec voo!" And ere the girl could protest, he had dismounted, turning the wall-eyed one's nose southward, and had delivered a resounding whack upon the rump of that temperamental animal.

"Allez! Go home! Beat it!" he cried.

The mule lost no time but headed for the distant corral at a canter; and Burley, grinning like a great, splendid, intelligent dog who has just done something to be proud of, stepped into the market cart and seated himself beside Maryette.

"Who told you where I am going?" she asked, scarcely knowing whether to laugh or let loose her indignation.

"Your father, Carillonnette."

"Why did you follow me?"

"I had nothing else to do——"

"Is that the reason?"

"I like to be with you——"

"Really, monsieur! And you think it was not necessary to consult my wishes?"

"Don't you like to be with me?" he asked, so naïvely that the girl blushed and bit her lip and shook the reins without replying.

They jogged on through the disused byway, the filbert bushes brushing axle and traces; but presently the little donkey relapsed into a walk again, and the girl, who had counted on that procedure when she started from Sainte Lesse, did not urge him.

"Also," she said in a low voice, "I have been wondering who permits you to address me as Carillonnette. Also as Maryette. You have been, heretofore, quite correct in assuming that mademoiselle is the proper form of address."

"I was so glad to see you," he said, so simply that she flushed again and offered no further comment.

For a long while she let him do the talking, which was perfectly agreeable to him. He talked on every subject he could think of, frankly practicing idioms on her, pleased with his own fluency and his progress in French.

After a while she said, looking around at him with a curiosity quite friendly:

"Tell me, Monsieur Burley, *why* did you desire to come with me today?"

He started to reply, but checked himself, looking into the dark blue and engaging eyes.

After a moment the engaging eyes became brilliantly serious.

"Tell me," she repeated. "Is it because there were some rumours last evening concerning Nivelle?"

"Wee!"

"Oh," she nodded, thoughtfully.

After driving for a little while in silence she looked around at him with an expression on her face which altered it exquisitely.

"Thank you, my friend," she murmured. . . . "And if you wish to call me Carillonnette —do so."

"I do want to. And my name's Jack. . . . If you don't mind."

Her eyes were fixed on her donkey's ears.

"Djack," she repeated, musingly. "Jacques —Djack—it's the same, isn't it—Djack?"

He turned red and she laughed at him, no longer afraid.

"Listen, my friend," she said, "it is *très beau*—what have you done."

"Vooz êtes tray belle——"

"*Non!* Please stop! It is not a question of me——"

"Vooz êtes tray chick——"

"Stop, Djack! That is not good manners! No! I was merely saying that—you have done something very nice. Which is quite true. You heard rumours that Nivelle had become unsafe. People whispered last evening —something about the danger of a salient being cut at its base. . . . I heard the gossip in the street. Was that why you came after me?"

"Wee."

"Thank you, Djack."

She leaned a trifle forward in the cart, her dimpled elbows on her knees, the reins sagging.

Blue and rosy jays flew up before them, fluttering away through the thickets; a bullfinch whistled sweetly from a thorn bush, watching them pass under him, unafraid.

"You see," she said, half to herself, "I *had* to come. Who could refuse our wounded? There is no bell-master in our department; and only one bell-mistress. . . . To find anyone else to play the Nivelle carillon one would have to pierce the barbarians' lines and search the ruins of Flanders for a *Beiaardier*—a *Klokkenist*, as they call a carillonneur in the low countries. . . . But the Mayor asked it, and our wounded are waiting. You understand, *mon ami* Djack, I had to come."

He nodded.

She added, naïvely:

"God watches over our trenches. We shall be quite safe in Nivelle."

A dull boom shook the sunlit air. Even in the cart they could feel the vibration.

An hour later, everywhere ahead of them, a vast, confused thundering was steadily increasing, deepening with every ominous reverberation.

Where two sandy wood roads crossed, a mounted gendarme halted them and examined their papers.

"My poor child," he said to the girl, shaking his head, "the wounded at Nivelle were taken away during the night. They are fighting there now in the streets."

"In Nivelle streets!" faltered the girl.

"*Oui, mademoiselle.* Of the carillon little remains. The Boches have been shelling it since daylight. Turn again. And it is better that you turn quickly, because it is not known to us what is going on in that wooded district over there. For if they get a foothold in Nivelle on this drive they might cross this road before evening."

The girl sat grief-stricken and silent in the cart, staring at the woods ahead where the road ran through taller saplings and where, here and there, mature trees towered.

All around them now the increasing thunder rolled and echoed and shook the ground under them. Half a dozen gendarmes came up at a gallop. Their officer drew bridle, seized the donkey's head and turned animal and cart southward.

"Go back," he said briefly, recognizing Burley and returning his salute. "You may have to take your mules out of Sainte Lesse!" he added, as he wheeled his horse. "We are getting into trouble out here, *nom de Dieu!*"

Maryette's head hung as the donkey jogged along, trotting willingly because his nose was now pointed homeward.

The girl drove with loose and careless rein

and in silence; and beside her sat Burley, his troubled gaze always reverting to the despondent form beside him.

"Too bad, little girl," he said. "But another time our wounded shall listen to your carillon."

"Never at Nivelle. . . . The belfry is being destroyed. . . . The sweetest carillon in France—the oldest, the most beautiful. . . . Fifty-six bells, Djack—a wondrous wilderness of bells rising above where one stands in the belfry, tier on tier, tier on tier, until one's gaze is lost amid the heavenly company aloft. . . . Oh, Djack! And the great bell, Clovis! He hangs there—through hundreds of years he has spoken with his great voice of God!— so that they heard him for miles and miles across the land——"

"Maryette—I am so sorry for you——"

"Oh! Oh! My carillon of Nivelle! My beloved carillon!"

"Maryette, dear! My little Carillonnette——"

"No—my heart is broken——"

"Vooz ates tray, tray belle——"

The sudden crashing of heavy feet in the bushes checked him; but it was too late to heed it now—too late to reach for his holster. For all around them swarmed the men in sea-grey, jerking the donkey off his forelegs, blocking the little wheels with great, dirty fists, seizing Burley from behind and dragging him violently out of the cart.

A near-sighted officer, thin and spare as Death, was talking in a loud, nasal voice and squinting at Burley where he still struggled, red and exasperated, in the clutches of four soldiers:

"Also! That is no uniform known to us or to any nation at war with us. That is not regulation in England—that collar insignia. This is a case of a franc-tireur! Now, then, you there in your costume de fantasie! What have you to say, eh?"

There was a silence; Burley ceased struggling.

"Answer, do you hear? What are you?"

"American."

"Pig-dog!" shouted the gaunt officer. "So you are one of those Yankee muleteers in your uniform, and armed! It is sufficient that you are American. If it had not been for America this war would be ended! But it is not enough, apparently, that you come here with munitions and food, that you insult us at sea, that you lie about us and slander us and send your shells and cartridges to England to slay our people! No! Also you must come to insult us in your clown's uniform and with your pistol—" The man began to choke with fury, unable to continue, except by gesture.

But the jerky gestures were terribly significant: soldiers were already pushing Burley across the road toward a great oak tree; six men fell out and lined up.

"M-my Government—" stammered the young fellow—but was given no opportunity to speak. Very white, the chill sweat standing on his forehead and under his eyes, he stood against the oak, lips compressed, grey eyes watching what was happening to him.

Suddenly he understood it was all over.

"Djack!"

He turned his gaze toward Maryette, where

she struggled toward him, held by two soldiers.

"Maryette—Carillonnette—" His voice suddenly became steady, perfectly clear. "*Je
vous aime*, Carillonnette."

"Oh, Djack! Djack!" she cried in terror.

He heard the orders; was aware of the
levelled rifles; but his reckless greyish eyes
were now fixed on her, and he began to laugh
almost mischievously.

"Vooz êtes tray belle," he said, "—tray,
tray chick——"

"Djack!"

But the clang of the volley precluded any
response from him except the half tender,
half reckless smile that remained on his youthful face where he lay looking up at the sky
with pleasant, sightless eyes, and a sunbeam
touching the metal mule on his blood-wet
collar.

CHAPTER XVII

She tried once more to lift the big, warm, flexible body, exerting all her slender strength. It was useless. It was like attempting to lift the earth. The weight of the body frightened her.

Again she sank down among the ferns under the great oak tree; once more she took his blood-smeared head on her lap, smoothing the bright, wet hair; and her tears fell slowly upon his upturned face.

"My friend," she stammered, "—my kind, droll friend. . . . The first friend I ever had——"

The gun thunder beyond Nivelle had ceased; an intense stillness reigned in the forest; only a leaf moved here and there on the aspens.

A few forest flies whirled about her, but

204

as yet no ominous green flies came—none of those jewelled harbingers of death which appear with horrible promptness and as though by magic from nowhere when anything dies in the open world.

Her donkey, still attached to the little gaily painted market cart, had wandered on up the sandy lane, feeding at random along the fern-bordered thickets which walled in the Nivelle byroad on either side.

Presently her ear caught a slight sound; something stirred somewhere in the woods behind her. After an interval of terrible stillness there came a distant crashing of footsteps among dead leaves and underbrush.

Horror of the Hun still possessed her; the victim of Prussian ferocity still lay across her knees. She dared not take the chance that friendly ears might hear her call for aid —dared not raise her voice in appeal lest she awaken something monstrous, unclean, inconceivable—the unseen thing which she could hear at intervals prowling there among dead leaves in the demi-light of the woods.

Suddenly her heart leaped with fright; a

man stepped cautiously out of the woods into the road; another, dressed in leather, with dry blood caked on his face, followed.

The first comer, a French gendarme, had already caught sight of the donkey and market cart; had turned around instinctively to look for their owner. Now he discovered her seated there among the ferns under the oak tree.

"In the name of God," he growled, "what's that child doing there!"

The airman in leather followed him across the road to the oak; the girl looked up at them out of dark, tear-marred eyes that seemed dazed.

"Well, little one!" rumbled the big, red-faced gendarme. "What's your name?—you who sit here all alone at the wood's edge with a dead man across your knees?"

She made an effort to find her voice—to control it.

"I am Maryette Courtray, bell-mistress of Sainte Lesse," she answered, trembling.

"And—this young man?"

"They shot him—the Prussians, monsieur."

206

"My poor child! Was he your lover, then?"

Her tear-filled eyes widened:

"Oh, no," she said naïvely; "it is sadder than that. He was my friend."

The big gendarme scratched his chin; then, with an odd glance at the young airman who stood beside him:

"To lose a friend is indeed sadder than to lose a lover. What was your friend's name, little one?"

She pressed her hand to her forehead in an effort to search among her partly paralyzed thoughts:

"Djack. . . . That is his name. . . . He was the first real friend I ever had."

The airman said:

"He is one of my countrymen—an American muleteer, Jack Burley—in charge at Sainte Lesse."

At the sound of the young man's name pronounced in English the girl began to cry. The big gendarme bent over and patted her cheek.

"*Allons*," he growled; "courage! little mistress of the bells! Let us place your friend in your pretty market cart and leave this accursed place, in God's name!"

He straightened up and looked over his shoulder.

"For the Boches are in Nivelle woods," he added, with an oath, "and we ought to be on our way to Sainte Lesse, if we are to arrive there at all. *Allons*, comrade, take him by the head!"

So the wounded airman bent over and took the body by the shoulders; the gendarme lifted the feet; the little bell-mistress followed, holding to one of the sagging arms, as though fearing that these strangers might take away from her this dead man who had been so much more to her than a mere lover.

When they laid him in the market cart she released his sleeve with a sob. Still crying, she climbed to the seat of the cart and gathered up the reins. Behind her, flat on the floor of the cart, the airman and the gendarme had seated themselves, with the young man's body between them. They were opening his tunic and shirt now and were whispering together, and wiping away blood from the naked shoulders and chest.

"He's still warm, but there's no pulse," whispered the airman. "He's dead enough, I guess, but I'd rather hear a surgeon say so."

The gendarme rose, stepped across to the seat, took the reins gently from the girl.

"Weep peacefully, little one," he said; "it does one good. Tears are the tisane which strengthens the soul."

"Ye-es. . . . But I am remembering that— that I was not very k-kind to him," she sobbed. "It hurts—*here*—" She pressed a slim hand over her breast.

"*Allons!* Friends quarrel. God understands. Thy friend back there—he also understands now."

"Oh, I hope he does! . . . He spoke to me so tenderly—yet so gaily. He was even laughing at me when they shot him. He was so kind—and droll—" She sobbed anew, clasping her hands and pressing them against her quivering mouth to check her grief.

"Was it an execution, then?" demanded the gendarme in his growling voice.

"They said he must be a franc-tireur to wear such a uniform——"

"Ah, the scoundrels! Ah, the assassins! And so they murdered him there under the tree?"

"Ah, God! Yes! I seem to see him standing there now—his grey, kind eyes—and no thought of fear—just a droll smile—the way he had with me——" whispered the girl, "the way—*his* way—with me——"

"Child," said the gendarme, pityingly, "it *was* love!"

But she shook her head, surprised, the tears still running down her tanned cheeks:

"Monsieur, it was more serious than love; it was friendship."

CHAPTER XVIII

Where the Fontanes highroad crosses the byroad to Sainte Lesse they were halted by a dusty column moving rapidly west—four hundred American mules convoyed by gendarmerie and remount troopers.

The sweating riders, passing at a canter, shouted from their saddles to the big gendarme in the market cart that neither Nivelle nor Sainte Lesse were to be defended at present, and that all stragglers were being directed to Fontanes and Le Marronnier. Mules and drivers defiled at a swinging trot, enveloped in torrents of white dust; behind them rode a peloton of the remount, lashing recalcitrant animals forward; and in the rear of these rolled automobile ambulances, red crosses aglow in the rays of the setting sun.

The driver of the last ambulance seemed to be ill; his head lay on the shoulder of a Sister of Charity who had taken the steering wheel.

The gendarme beside Maryette signalled her to stop; then he got out of the market cart and, lifting the body of the American muleteer in his powerful arms, strode across the road. The airman leaped from the market cart and followed him.

Between them they drew out a stretcher, laid the muleteer on it, and shoved it back into the vehicle.

There was a brief consultation, then they both came back to Maryette, who, rigid in her seat and very pale, sat watching the procedure in silence.

The gendarme said:

"I go to Fontanes. There's a dressing station on the road. It appears that your young man's heart hasn't quite stopped yet——"

The girl rose excitedly to her feet, but the gendarme gently forced her back into her seat and laid the reins in her hands. To the airman he growled:

"I did not tell this poor child to hope; I merely informed her that her friend yonder is still breathing. But he's as full of holes as a pepper pot!" He frowned at Maryette: "*Allons!* My comrade here goes to Sainte Lesse. Drive him there now, in God's name, before the Uhlans come clattering on your heels!"

He turned, strode away to the ambulance once more, climbed in, and placed one big arm around the sick driver's shoulder, drawing the man's head down against his breast.

"*Bonne chance!*" he called back to the airman, who had now seated himself beside Maryette. "Explain to our little bell-mistress that we're taking her friend to a place where they fool Death every day—where to cheat the grave is a flourishing business! Goodbye! Courage! En route, brave Sister of the World!"

The Sister of Charity turned and smiled at Maryette, made her a friendly gesture, threw in the clutch, and, twisting the steering wheel with both sun-browned hands, guided the machine out onto the road and sped away swiftly after the cloud of receding dust.

"Drive on, mademoiselle," said the airman quietly.

In his accent there was something poignantly familiar to Maryette, and she turned with a start and looked at him out of her dark blue, tear-marred eyes.

"Are *you* also American?" she asked.

"Gunner observer, American air squadron, mademoiselle."

"An airman?"

"Yes. My machine was shot down in Nivelle woods an hour ago."

After a silence, as they jogged along between the hazel thickets in the warm afternoon sunshine:

"Were you acquainted with my friend?" she asked wistfully.

"With Jack Burley? A little. I knew him in Calais."

The tears welled up into her eyes:

"Could you tell me about him? . . . He was my first friend. . . . I did not understand him in the beginning, monsieur. Among children it is different; I had known boys—as one knows them at school. But a man, never—and, indeed, I had not thought I had grown up until—he came—Djack—to live at our inn. . . . The White Doe at Sainte Lesse, monsieur. My father keeps it."

"I see," nodded the airman gravely.

"Yes—that is the way. He came—my first friend, Djack—with mules from America, monsieur—one thousand mules. And God knows Sainte Lesse had never seen the like! As for me—I thought I was a child still—until—do you understand, monsieur?"

"Yes, Maryette."

"Yes, that is how I found I was grown up. He was a man, not a boy—that is how I found out. So he became my first friend. He was quite droll, and very big and kind—and timid —following me about—oh, it was quite droll for both of us, because at first I was afraid, but pretended not to be."

She smiled, then suddenly her eyes filled with the tragedy again, and she began to whimper softly to herself, with a faint sound like a hovering pigeon.

"Tell me about him," said the airman.

She staunched her tears with the edge of her apron.

"It was that way with us," she managed to say. "I was enchanted and a little frightened —it being my first friendship. He was so big, so droll, so kind. . . . We were on our way to Nivelle this morning. I was to play the carillon—being mistress of the bells at Sainte Lesse—and there was nobody else to play the bells at Nivelle; and the wounded desired to hear the carillon."

"Yes."

"So Djack came after me—hearing rumours of Prussians in that direction. They were true—oh, God!—and the Prussians caught us there where you found us."

She bowed her supple figure double on the seat, covering her face with her sun-browned hands.

The airman drove on, whistling "La Brabançonne" under his breath, and deep in thought. From time to time he glanced at the curved figure beside him; but he said no more for a long time.

Toward sunset they drove into the Sainte Lesse highway.

He spoke abruptly, dryly:

"Anybody can weep for a friend. But few avenge their dead."

She looked up, bewildered.

They drove under the old Sainte Lesse gate as he spoke. The sunlight lay pink across the walls and tipped the turret of the watch tower with fire.

The town seemed very still; nothing was to be seen on the long main street except here and there a Spahi horseman *en vidette*, and the clock-tower pigeons circling in their evening flight.

The girl, Maryette, looked dumbly into the fading daylight when the cart stopped before her door. The airman took her gently by the arm, and that awakened her. As though stiffened by fatigue she rose and climbed to the sidewalk. He took her unresisting arm and led her through the tunnelled wall and into the White Doe Inn.

"Get me some supper," he said. "It will take your mind off your troubles."

217

"Yes."

"Bread, wine, and some meat, if you have any. I'll be back in a few moments."

He left her at the inn door and went out into the street, whistling "La Brabançonne." A cavalryman directed him to the military telephone installed in the house of the notary across the street.

His papers identified him; the operator gave him his connection; they switched him to the headquarters of his air squadron, where he made his report.

"Shot down?" came the sharp exclamation over the wire.

"Yes, sir, about eleven-thirty this morning on the north edge of Nivelle forest."

"The machine?"

"Done for, sir. They have it."

"You?"

"A scratch—nothing. I had to run."

"What else have you to report?"

The airman made his brief report in an unemotional voice. Ending it, he asked permission to volunteer for a special service. And for ten minutes the officer at the other end of the wire listened to a proposition which interested him intensely.

When the airman finished, the officer said:
"Wait till I relay this matter."

For a quarter of an hour the airman waited. Finally the operator half turned on his camp chair and made a gesture for him to resume the receiver.

"If you choose to volunteer for such service," came the message, "it is approved. But understand—you are not ordered on such duty."

"I understand. I volunteer."

"Very well. Munitions go to you immediately by automobile. It is expected that the wind will blow from the west by morning. By morning, also, all reserves will arrive in the west salient. What is to be your signal?"

"The carillon from the Nivelle belfry."

"What tune?"

" 'La Brabançonne.' If not that, then the tocsin on the great bell, Clovis."

In the tiny café the crippled innkeeper sat, his aged, wistful eyes watching three leather-clad airmen who had been whispering together around a table in the corner all the afternoon.

They nodded in silence to the new arrival, and he joined them.

Daylight faded in the room; the drum in the Sainte Lesse belfry, set to play before the hour sounded, began to turn aloft; the silvery notes of the carillon seemed to shower down from the sky, filling the twilight world with angelic melody. Then, in resonant beauty, the great bell, Bayard, measured the hour.

The airman who had just arrived went to a sink, washed the caked blood from his face and tied it up with a first-aid bandage. Then he began to pace the café, his head bent in thought, his nervous hands clasped behind him.

The room was dusky when he came back to the table where his three comrades still sat consulting in whispers. The old innkeeper had fallen asleep on his chair by the window. There was no light in the room except what came from stars.

"Well," said one of the airmen in a carefully modulated voice, "what are you going to do, Jim?"

"Stay."

"What's the idea?"

The bandaged airman rested both hands on the stained table-top:

"We quit Nivelle tonight, but our reserves are already coming up and we are to retake Nivelle tomorrow. You flew over the town this morning, didn't you?"

All three said yes.

"You took photographs?"

"Certainly."

"Then you know that our trenches pass under the bell-tower?"

"Yes."

"Very well. The wind is north. When the Boches enter our trenches they'll try to gas our salient while the wind holds. But west winds are predicted after sunrise tomorrow. I'm going to get into the Nivelle belfry tonight with a sack of bombs. I'm going to try to explode their gas cylinders if I can. The tocsin is the signal for our people in the salient."

"You're crazy!" remarked one of the airmen.

"No; I'll bluff it out. I'm to have a Boche uniform in a few moments."

"You *are* crazy! You know what they'll do to you, don't you, Jim?"

The bandaged airman laughed, but in his eyes there was an odd flicker like a tiny flame. He whistled "La Brabançonne" and glanced coolly about the room.

One of the airmen said to another in a whisper:

"There you are. Ever since they got his brother he's been figuring on landing a whole bunch of Huns at one clip. This is going to finish him, this business."

Another said:

"Don't try anything like that, Jim——"

"Sure, I'll try it," interrupted the bandaged airman pleasantly. "When are you fellows going?"

"Now."

"All right. Take my report. Wait a moment——"

"For God's sake, Jim, act sensibly!"

The bandaged airman laughed, fished out from his clothing somewhere a note book and pencil. One of the others turned an electric torch on the table; the bandaged man made a little sketch, wrote a few lines which the others studied.

"You can get that note to headquarters in half an hour, can't you, Ed?"

"Yes."

"All right. I'll wait here for my answer."

"You know what risk you run, Jim?" pleaded the youngest of the airmen.

"Oh, certainly. All right, then. You'd better be on your way."

After they had left the room, the bandaged airman sat beside the table, thinking hard in the darkness.

Presently from somewhere across the dusky river meadow the sudden roar of an airplane engine shattered the silence; then another whirring racket broke out; then another.

He heard presently the loud rattle of his

comrades' machines from high above him in the star-set sky; he heard the stertorous breathing of the old innkeeper; he heard again the crystalline bell-notes break out aloft, linger in linked harmonies, die away; he heard Bayard's mellow thunder proclaim the hour once more.

There was a watch on his wrist, but it had been put out of business when his machine fell in Nivelle woods. Glancing at it mechanically he saw the phosphorescent dial glimmer faintly under shattered hands that remained fixed.

An hour later Bayard shook the starlit silence ten times.

As the last stroke boomed majestically through the darkness an automobile came racing into the long, unlighted street of Sainte Lesse and halted, panting, at the door of the White Doe Inn.

The airman went out to the doorstep, saluted the staff captain who leaned forward from the tonneau and turned a flash on him. Then, satisfied, the officer lifted a bundle from the tonneau and handed it to the airman. A letter was pinned to the bundle.

After the airman had read the letter twice, the staff captain leaned a trifle nearer.

"Do you think it can be done?" he demanded bluntly.

"Yes, sir."

"Very well. Here are your munitions, too."

He lifted from the tonneau a bomb-thrower's sack, heavy and full. The airman took it and saluted.

"It means the cross," said the staff captain dryly. And to the engineer chauffeur: "Let loose!"

CHAPTER XIX

HONOUR

For a moment the airman stood watching and listening. The whir of the receding car died away in the night.

Then, carrying his bundle and his bomber's sack, heavy with latent death, he went into the inn and through the café, where the sleeping innkeeper sat huddled, and felt his way cautiously to the little dining room.

The wooden shutters had been closed; a candle flared on the table. Maryette sat beside it, her arms extended across the cloth, her head bowed.

He thought she was asleep, but she looked up as his footfall sounded on the bare floor.

She was so pale that he asked her if she felt ill.

"No. I have been thinking of my friend," she replied in a low but steady voice.

"He may live," said the airman. "He was alive when we lifted him."

The girl nodded as though preoccupied— an odd, mysterious little nod, as though assenting to some intimate, inward suggestion of her own mind.

Then she raised her dark blue eyes to the airman, who was still standing beside the table, the sack of bombs hanging from his left shoulder, the bundle under his arm.

"Here is supper," she said, looking around absently at the few dishes. Then she folded her hands on the table's edge and sat silent, as though lost in thought.

He placed the sack carefully on a cane chair beside him, the bundle on the floor, and seated himself opposite her. There was bread, meat, and a bottle of red wine. The girl declined to eat, saying that she had supped.

"Your friend Jack," he said again, after a long silence, "—I have seen worse cases. He may live, mademoiselle."

"That," she said musingly, in her low, even

voice, "is now in God's hands." She gave
the slightest movement to her shoulders, as
though easing them a trifle of that burden.
"I have prayed. You saw me weep. That is
ended—so much. Now—" and across her eyes
shot a blue gleam, "—now I am ready to listen to *you!* In the cart—out on the road
there—you said that anybody can weep, but
that few dare avenge."

"Yes," he drawled, "I said that."

"Very well, then; tell me *how!*"

"What do *you* want to avenge? Your
friend?"

"His country's honour, and mine! If he
had been slain—otherwise—I should have perhaps mourned him, confident in the law of
France. But—I have seen the Rhenish swine
on French soil—I saw the Boches do this
thing in France. It is not merely my friend
I desire to avenge; it is the triple crime
against his life, against the honour of his
country and of mine." She had not raised
her voice; had not stirred in her chair.

The airman, who had stopped eating, sat

228

with fork in hand, listening, regarding her intently.

"Yes," he said, resuming his meal, "I understand quite well what you mean. Some such philosophy sent my elder brother and me over here from New York—the wild hogs trampling through Belgium—the ferocious herds from the Rhine defacing, defiling, rending, obliterating all that civilized man has reverenced for centuries. . . . That's the idea — the world-wide menace of these unclean hordes—and the murderous filth of them! . . . They got my brother."

He shrugged, realizing that his face had flushed with the heat of inner fires.

"Coolness does it," he added, almost apologetically, "—method and coolness. The world must keep its head clear: yellow fever and smallpox have been nearly stamped out; the Hun can be eliminated—with intelligence and clear thinking. . . . And I'm only an American airman who has been shot down like a winged heron whose comrades have lingered a little to comfort him and have gone on. . . . Yes, but a winged heron can still stab, little mistress of the bells. . . . And every blow counts. . . . Listen attentively—for Jack's sake . . . and for the sake of France. For I am going to explain to you how you can strike— if you want to."

"I am listening," said Maryette serenely.

"We may not live through it. Even my orders do not send me to do this thing; they merely permit it. Are you contented to go with me?"

She nodded, the shadow of a smile on her lips.

"Very well. You play the carillon?"

"Yes."

"You can play 'La Brabançonne'?"

"Yes."

"On the bells?"

"Yes."

He rose, went around the table, carrying his chair with him, and seated himself beside her. She inclined her pale, pretty head; he placed his lips close to her ear, speaking very slowly and distinctly, explaining his plan in every minute detail.

While he was still speaking in a whisper,

the street outside filled with the trample of arriving cavalry. The Spahis were leaving the environs of Sainte Lesse; *chasseurs à cheval* followed from still farther afield, escorting ambulances from the Nivelle hospitals now being abandoned.

"The trenches at Nivelle are being emptied," said the airman.

"And do you mean that you and I are to go there, to Nivelle?" she asked.

"That is exactly what I mean. In an hour I shall be in the Nivelle belfry. Will you be there with me?"

"Yes."

"Excellent!" he exclaimed. "You can play 'La Brabançonne' on the bells while I blow hell out of them in the redoubt below us!"

The infantry from the Nivelle trenches began to pass. There were a few wagons, a battery of seventy-fives, a soup kitchen or two and a long column of mules from Fontanes.

Two American muleteers knocked at the inn door and came stamping into the hallway, asking for a loaf and a bottle of red wine. Maryette rose from the table to find provisions; the airman got up also, saying in English:

"Where do you come from, boys?"

"From Fontanes corral," they replied, surprised to hear their own tongue spoken.

"Do you know Jack Burley, one of your people?"

"Sure. He's just been winged bad."

"The Huns done him up something fierce," added the other.

"Very bad?"

Maryette came back with a loaf and two bottles.

"I seen him at Fontanes," replied the muleteer, taking the provisions from the girl. "He's all shot to pieces, but they say he'll pull through."

The airman turned to Maryette:

"Jack will get well," he translated bluntly.

The girl, who had just refused the money offered by the American muleteer, turned sharply, became deadly white for a second, then her face flamed with a hot and splendid colour.

One of the muleteers said:

"Is this here his girl?"

"Yes," nodded the airman.

The muleteer became voluble, patting Maryette on one arm and then on the other:

"J'ai vue Jack Burley, mamzelle, toot a l'heure! Il est bien, savvy voo! Il est tray, tray bien! Bocoo de trou! N'importe! I'l va tray bien! Savvy voo? Jack Burley, l'ami de voo! Comprenny? On va le guerir toot sweet! Wee! Wee! Wee!——"

The girl flung her arms around the amazed muleteer's neck and kissed him impetuously on both cheeks. The muleteer blushed and his comrade fidgeted. Only the girl remained unembarrassed.

Half laughing, half crying, terribly excited, and very lovely to look upon, she caught both muleteers by their sleeves and poured out a torrent of questions. With the airman's aid she extracted what information they had to offer; and they went their way, flustered, still blushing, clasping bread and bottles to their agitated breasts.

The airman looked her keenly in the eyes as she came back from the door, still intensely excited, adorably transfigured. She opened her lips to speak—the happy exclamation on her lips, already half uttered, died there.

"Well?" inquired the airman quietly.

Dumb, still breathing rapidly, she returned his gaze in silence.

"Now that your friend Jack is going to live —what next?" asked the airman pleasantly.

For a full minute she continued to stare at him without a word.

"No need to avenge him now," added the airman, watching her.

"No." She turned, gazed vaguely into space. After a moment she said, as though to herself: "But his country's honour—and mine? That reckoning still remains! Is it not true?"

The airman said, with a trace of pity in his voice, for the girl seemed very young:

"You need not go with me to Nivelle just because you promised."

"Oh," she said simply, "I must go, of course—it being a question of our country's honour."

"I do not ask it. Nor would Jack, your

friend. Nor would your own country ask it of you, Maryette Courtray."

She replied serenely:

"But *I* ask it—of *myself*. Do you understand, monsieur?"

"Perfectly." He glanced mechanically at his useless wrist watch, then inquired the time. She went to her room, returned, wearing a little jacket and carrying a pair of big, wooden gloves.

"It is after eleven o'clock," she said. "I brought my jacket because it is cold in all belfries. It will be cold in Nivelle, up there in the tower under Clovis."

"You really mean to go with me?"

She did not even trouble to reply to the question. So he picked up his packet and his sack of bombs, and they went out, side by side, under the tunnelled wall.

Infantry from Nivelle trenches were still plodding along the dark street under the trees; dull gleams came from their helmets and bayonets in the obscure light of the stars.

The girl stood watching them for a few

moments, then her hand sought the airman's arm:

"If there is to be a battle in the street here, my father cannot remain."

The airman nodded, went out into the street and spoke to a passing officer. He, in turn, signalled the driver of a motor omnibus to halt.

The little bell-mistress entered the tavern, followed by two soldiers. In a few moments they came out bearing, chair-fashion between them, the crippled innkeeper.

The old man was much alarmed, but his daughter followed beside him to the omnibus, in which were several lamed soldiers.

"*Et toi?*" he quavered as they lifted him in. "What of thee, Maryette?"

"I follow," she called out cheerily. "I rejoin thee—" the bus moved on—"God knows when or where!" she added under her breath.

The airman was whispering to a fat staff officer when she rejoined him. All three looked up in silence at the belfry of Sainte Lesse, looming above them, a monstrous shadow athwart the stars. A moment later

an automobile, arriving from the south, drew
up in front of the inn.

"*Bonne chance*," said the fat officer
abruptly; he turned and waddled swiftly away
in the darkness. They saw him mount his
horse. His legs stuck out sideways.

"Now," whispered the airman, with a nod
to the chauffeur.

The little bell-mistress entered the car, her
wooden gloves tucked under one arm. The
airman followed with his packet and his sack
of bombs. The chauffeur started his engine.

The middle of the road was free to him;
the edges were occupied by the retreating infantry. As the car started, very slowly, cautiously feeling its way out of Sainte Lesse,
the fat staff officer turned his horse and
trotted up alongside. The car stopped, the
engine still running.

"It's understood?" asked the officer in a low
voice. "It's to be when we hear 'La Brabançonne'?"

"When you hear 'La Brabançonne.' "

"Understood," said the staff officer crisply,
saluted and drew bridle. And the car moved

out into the starlit night along an endless column of retreating soldiers, who were laughing, smoking, and chatting as though not in the least depressed by their withdrawal from the dry and cosy trenches of Nivelle which they were abandoning.

CHAPTER XX

"LA BRABANÇONNE"

No shells were falling in Nivelle as they left the car on the outskirts of the town and entered the long main street. That was all of Nivelle, a long, treeless main street from which branched a few alleys.

Smouldering débris of what had been houses illuminated the street. There were no other lights. Nothing stirred except a gaunt cat flitting like a shadow along the gutter. There was not a sound save the faint stirring of the cinders over which pale flames played fitfully.

Abandoned trenches ditched the little town in every direction; temporary shelters made of boughs, sheds, and broken-down wagons stood along the street. Otherwise, all impedimenta, materials, and stores had apparently been removed by the retreating columns. There was little wreckage except the burning débris of the few shell-struck houses—a few rags, a few piles of firewood, a bundle of straw and hay here and there.

High, mounting toward the stars, the ancient tower with its gilded hippogriff dominated the place—a vast, vague shape brooding over the single mile-long street and grimy alleys branching from it.

Nobody guarded the portal; the ancient doors stood wide open; pitch darkness reigned within.

"Do you know the way?" whispered the airman.

"Yes. Take hold of my hand."

He dared not use his flash. Carrying bundle and bombsack under one arm, he sought for her hand and encountered it. Cool, slim fingers closed over his.

After a few moments' stealthy advance, she whispered:

"Here are the stairs. Be careful; they twist."

She started upward, feeling with her feet

for every stone step. The ascent appeared to be interminable; the narrowing stone spiral seemed to have no end. Her hand grew warm within his own.

But at last they felt a fresh wind blowing and caught a glimpse of stars above them.

Then, tier on tier, the bells of the carillon, fixed to their great beams, appeared above them—a shadowy, bewildering wilderness of bells, rising, rank above rank, until they vanished in the darkness overhead. Beside them, almost touching them, loomed the great bell Clovis, a gigantic mass bulking enormously in that shadowy place.

A sonorous wind flowed through the open tower, eddying among the bells—a strong, keen night wind blowing from the north.

The airman walked to the south parapet and looked down. Below him in the starlight, like an indistinct map spread out, lay the Nivelle redoubt and the trench with its gabions, its sand bags, its timbers, its dugouts.

Very far away to the southeast they could see the glare of rockets and exploding shells, but the sound of the bombardment did not reach them. North, a single searchlight played and switched across the clouds; west, all was dark.

"They'll arrive just before dawn," said the airman, placing his sack of bombs on the pavement under the parapet. "Come, little bell-mistress, take me to see your keyboard."

"It is below—a few steps. This way—if you will follow me——"

She turned to the stone stairs again, descended a dozen steps, opened a door on a narrow landing.

And there, in the starlight, he saw the keyboard and the bewildering maze of wires running up and branching like a huge web toward the tiers of bells above.

He looked at the keyboard curiously. The little mistress of the bells displayed the two wooden gloves with which she encased her hands when she played the carillon.

"It would be impossible for one to play unless one's hands are armoured," she explained.

"It is almost a lost art," he mused aloud, "—this playing the carillon—this wonderful bell-music of the middle ages. There are few great bell-masters in this day."

"Few," she said dreamily.

"And"—he turned and stared at her—"few mistresses of the bells, I imagine."

"I think I am the only one in France or in Flanders. . . . And there are few carillons left. The Huns are battering them down. Towers of the ancient ages are falling everywhere in Flanders and in France under their shell fire. Very soon there will be no more of the old carillons left; no more bell-music in the world." She sighed heavily. "It is a pity."

She seated herself at the keyboard.

"Dare I play?" she asked, looking up over her shoulder.

"No; it would only mean a shell from the Huns."

She nodded, laid the wooden gloves beside her and let her delicate hands wander over the mute keys.

Leaning beside her the airman quietly explained the plan they were to follow.

"With dawn they will come creeping into

Nivelle—the Huns," he said. "I have one of their officers' uniforms in that bundle above. I shall try to pass as a general officer. You see, I speak German. My education was partly ruined in Germany. So I'll get on very well, I expect.

"And directly under us is the trench and the main redoubt. They'll occupy that first thing. They'll swarm there—the whole trench will be crawling with them. They'll install their gas cylinders at once, this wind being their wind.

"But with sunrise the wind changes—and whether it changes or not, I don't care," he added. "I've got them at last where I want them."

The girl looked up at him. He smiled that terrifying smile of his:

"With the explosion of my first bomb among their gas cylinders you are to start these bells above us. Are you afraid?"

"No."

"You are to play 'La Brabançonne.' That is the signal to our trenches."

"I have often played it," she said coolly.

"Not in the teeth of a barbarian army. Not in the faces of a murderous soldiery."

The girl sat quite still for a few moments; then looking up at him, and very pale in the starlight:

"Do you think they will tear me to pieces, monsieur?"

He said:

"I mean to hold those stairs with my sack of bombs until our people enter the trenches. If they can do it in an hour we will be all right."

"Yes."

"It is only a half-hour affair from our salient. I allow our people an hour."

"Yes."

"But if, even now, you had rather go back——"

"*No!*"

"There is no disgrace in going back."

"You said once, 'anybody can weep for friend and country. Few avenge either.' I am—happy—to be among the few."

He nodded. After a moment he said:

"I'll bet you something. My country is all

right, but it's sick. It's got a nauseous dose
of verbiage to spew up—something it's swallowed—something about being too proud to
fight. . . . My brother and I couldn't stand
it, so we came to France. . . . He was in the
photo air service. He was in mufti—and
about two miles up, I believe. Six Huns went
for him. . . . And winged him. He had to
land behind their lines. . . . In mufti. . . .
Well—I've never found courage to hear the
details. I can't stand them—yet."

"Your brother—is dead, monsieur?" she
asked timidly.

"Oh, yes. With—circumstances. Well, then
—after that, from an ordinary, commonplace
man I became a machine for the extermination
of vermin. That's all I am—an animated maga-
zine of Persian powder—or I do it in any
handy way. It's not a sporting proposition,
you see, just get rid of them any old way.
You don't understand, do you?"

"A—little."

"But it's slow work—slow work," he muttered vaguely, "—and the world is crawling—
crawling with them. But if God guides my

bomb this time and if I hit one of their gas cylinders—*that* ought to be worth while."

In the starlight his features became tense and terrible; she shivered in her threadbare jacket.

After a few moments' silence he went away up the steps to put on his German uniform. When he descended again she had a troubled question for him to answer:

"But how shall you account for me, a French girl, monsieur, if they come to the belfry?"

A heavy flush darkened his face:

"Little mistress of the bells, I shall pretend to be what the Huns are. Do you know how they treat French women?"

"I have heard," she said faintly.

"Then if they come and find you here as my—*prisoner*—they will think they understand."

The colour flamed in her face and she bowed it, resting her elbows on the keyboard.

"Come," he said, "don't be distressed. Does it matter what a Hun thinks? Come; let's be cheerful. Can you hum for me 'La Brabançonne'?"

She did not reply.

"Well, never mind," he said. "But it's a grand battle anthem. . . . We Americans have one. . . . It's out of fashion. And after all, I had rather hear 'La Brabançonne' when the time comes. . . . What a terrible admission! But what Americans have done to my country is far more terrible. The nation's sick—sick! . . . I prefer 'La Brabançonne' for the time being."

The Prussians entered Nivelle a little before dawn. The airman had been watching the street below. Down there in the slight glow from the cinders of what once had been a cottage a cat had been squatting, staring at the bed of coals, as though she were once more installed upon the family hearthstone.

Then something unseen as yet by the airman attracted the animal's attention. Alert, crouching, she stared down the vista of dark, deserted houses, then turned and fled like a ghost.

For a long while the airman perceived nothing. Suddenly close to the house façades on either side of the street, shadowy forms came gliding forward.

They passed the glowing embers and went on toward Sainte-Lesse; jägers, with knapsacks on back and rifles trailing; and on their heads oddly shaped pot helmets with battered looking visors.

One or two motorcyclists followed, whizzing through the desolate street and into the country beyond.

After a few minutes, out of the throat of the darkness emerged a solid column of infantry. In a moment, beneath the bell tower, the ground was swarming with Huns; every inch of the earth became infested with them; fields, hedges, alleys crawled alive with Germans. They overran every road, every street, every inch of open country; their wagons choked the main thoroughfare, they were already establishing themselves in the redoubt below, in the trench, running in and out of dugouts and all over scarp, counter-scarp, parades and parapet, ant-like in energy, busy with machine gun, trench mortar, installing telephones, searchlights, periscopes, machine guns.

Automobiles arrived—two armoured cars and grey passenger machines in which there were officers.

The airman laid his hand on Maryette's arm.

"Little bell-mistress," he said, "German officers are coming into the tower. I want them to find you in my arms when they come up into this belfry. Understand me, and forgive me."

"I—understand," she whispered.

"Play your part bravely. Will you?"

"Yes."

He put his arms around her; they stood rigid, listening.

"Now!" he whispered, and drew her close, kissing her.

Spurred boots clattered on the stone floor:

"Herr Je!" exclaimed an astonished voice. Somebody laughed. But the airman coolly pushed the girl aside, and as the faint grey light of dawn fell on his field uniform bearing the ribbon of the iron cross, two pairs of spurred heels hastily clinked together and two hands flew to the oddly shaped helmet visors.

"Also!" exclaimed the airman in a mincing

Berlin accent. "When I require a corps of observers I usually send my aide. That being now quite perfectly understood, you gentlemen will give yourselves the trouble to descend as you have come. Further, you will place a sentry at the tower door, and inform enquirers that General Count von Gierdorff and his staff are occupying the Nivelle belfry for purposes of observation."

The astounded officers saluted steadily; and if they imagined that the mythical staff of this general officer was clustered aloft somewhere up there where the bells hung it was impossible to tell by the strained expressions on their wooden countenances.

However, it was evidently perfectly plain to them what the high Excellenz was about in this vaulted room where wires led aloft to an unseen carillon on the landing in the belfry above.

The airman nodded; they went. And when their clattering steps echoed far below on the spiral stone stairs, the airman motioned to the little bell-mistress. She followed him up the short flight to where the bells hung.

"We're in for it now," he said. "If High Command comes into this place to investigate then I shall have to hold those stairs. . . . It's growing quite light in the east. Which way is the wind?"

"North," she said in a steady voice. She was terribly pale.

He went to the parapet and looked over, half wondering, perhaps, whether he would receive a rifle shot through the head.

Far below at the foot of the bell-tower the dimly discerned Nivelle redoubt, swarming with men, was being armed; and, to the south, wired he thought, but could not see distinctly.

Then, as the dusk of early dawn grew greyer, the first rifle shots rattled out in the west. The French salient was saluting the wire-stringers.

Back under shelter they tumbled; whistles sounded distantly; a trench mortar crashed; then the accentless tattoo of machine guns broke from every emplacement.

"The east is turning a little yellow," he said calmly. "I believe this matter is going through.

Toss some dust into the air. Which way?"

"North," said the girl.

"Good. I think they're placing their cylinders. I think I can see them laying their coils. I'm certain of it. What luck!"

The airman was becoming excited and his voice trembled a little with the effort to control it.

"It's growing pink in the east. Try a handful of dust again," he suggested almost gaily.

"North," she said briefly, watching the dust aloft.

"Luck's with us! Look at the east! If their High Command keeps his nose out of this place!—if he *does*!—Look at the east, little bell-mistress! It's all gold! There's pink up higher. I can see a faint tinge of blue, too. Can you?"

"I think so."

A minute dragged like a year in prison. Then:

"Try the wind again," he said in a strained voice.

"North."

"Oh, luck! Luck!" he muttered, slinging his

sack of bombs over his shoulder. "We've got them! We've certainly got them! What's that! An airplane! Look, little girl—one of our planes is up. There's another! Which way is the wind?"

"North."

"Got 'em!" he snapped between his teeth. "Run over to the stairs. Listen! Is anybody coming up?"

"I can hear nothing."

"Stand there and listen. Never mind the row the guns are making; listen for somebody on the stairs. Look how light it's getting! The sun will push up before many minutes. We've got 'em! *Got 'em!* Wet your finger and try the wind!"

"North."

"North here, too. What do you know about that! Luck! Luck's with us! And we've got 'em—!" he lifted his clenched hand and laughed at her. "Like that!" he said, his blue eyes blazing. "They're getting ready to gas below. Look at 'em! Glory to God! I can see two cylinders directly under me. They're manning the nozzles! Every man is masking at his post! Anybody on the stairs! Any sound?"

"None."

"Are you certain?"

"It is as still as death below."

"Try the dust. The wind's changing, I think. Quick! Which way?"

"*West.*"

"Oh, glory! Glory to God! They feel it below! They know. The wind has changed. Off came their respirators. No gas this morning, eh? Yes, by God, there will be gas enough for all——!"

He caught up a bomb, leaned over the parapet, held it aloft, poised, aiming steadily for one second of concentrated coördination of mind and muscle. Then straight down he launched it. The cylinder beneath him was shattered and a green geyser of gas burst from it deluging the trench.

Already a second bomb followed the first, then another, and then a third; and with the last report another cylinder in the trench below burst into thick green billows of death and flowed over the ground, *west.*

Two more bombs whirled down, bursting on a machine gun; then the airman turned with a cry of triumph, and at the same instant the sun rose above the hills and flung a golden ray straight across his face.

To Maryette the man stood transfigured, like the Blazing Guardian of the Flaming Sword.

"Ring out your Brabançonne!" he cried. "Let the Huns hear the war song of the land they've trampled! Now! Little bell-mistress, arm your white hands with your wooden gloves and make this old carillon speak in brass and iron!"

He caught her by the arm; they ran down the short flight of steps; she drew on her wooden gloves and sprang to the keyboard.

"I'll hold the stairs!" he cried. "I can hold these stairs for an hour against the whole world in arms. Now, then! The Brabançonne!"

Above the roaring confusion and the explosions far below, from high up in the sky a clear bell note floated as though out of Heaven itself—another, others, crystalline clear, imperious, filling all the sky with their amazing and terrible beauty.

The mistress of the bells struck the keyboard with armoured hands—beautiful, slender, avenging hands; the bells above her crashed out into the battle-song of Flanders, filling sky and earth with its splendid defiance of the Hun.

The airman, bomb in hand, stood at the head of the stone stairs; the ancient tower rocked with the fiercely magnificent anthem of revolt—the war cry of a devastated land —the land that died to save the world—the martyr, Belgium, still prone in the deathly trance awaiting her certain resurrection.

The rising sun struck the tower where three score ancient bells poured from metal throats their heavenly summons to battle!

The Hun heard it, tumbling, clawing, strangling below in the hellish vapours of his own death-fog; and now, from the rear his sky-guns hurled shrapnel at the carillon in the belfry of Nivelle.

Clouds possessed the tower—soft, white, fleecy clouds rolling, unfolding, floating about

the ancient buttresses and gargoyles. An iron
hail rained on slate and parapet and resounding bell-metal. But the bells pealed and pealed
in clear-voiced beauty, and Clovis, the great
iron giant, hung, scarcely sonorous under the
shrapnel rain.

Suddenly there were bayonets on the stairs
—the clatter of heavy feet—alien faces on the
threshold. Then a bomb flew, and the terrible
crash cleared the stairs.

Twice more the clatter came with the clank
of bayonets and guttural cries; but both died
out in the infernal roar of the grenades exploding inside that stony spiral. And no more
bayonets flickered on the stairs.

The airman, frozen to a statue, listened.
Again and again he thought he could hear
bugles, but the roar from below blotted out
the distant call.

"Little bell-mistress!"

She turned her head, her hands still striking
the keyboard. He spoke through the confusion of the place:

"Sound the tocsin!"

Then Clovis thundered from the belfry like

a great gun fired, booming out over the world. Around the iron colossus shrapnel swept in gusts; Clovis thundered on, annihilating all sound except his own tremendous voice, heedless of shell and bullet, disdainful of the hell's shambles below, where masked French infantry were already leaping the parapets of Nivelle Redoubt into the squirming masses below.

The airman shouted at her through the tumult:

"They murdered my brother. Did I tell you? They hacked him to slivers with their bayonets. I've settled the reckoning down in the gas there—their own green gas, damn them! You don't understand what I say, do you? He was my brother——"

A frightful explosion blew in the oubliette; the room rattled and clattered with shrapnel.

The airman swayed where he stood in the swirling smoke, lurched up against the stone coping, slid down to his knees.

When his eyes opened the little bell-mistress was bending over him.

"They got me," he gasped. All the front of his tunic was sopping red.

"They said it meant the cross—if I made good. . . . Are you hurt?"

"Oh, no!" she whispered. "But you——"

"Go on and play!" he whispered with a terrible effort.

"But you——"

"The Brabançonne! Quick!"

She went, whimpering. Standing before the keyboard she pulled on her wooden gloves and struck the keys.

Out over the infernal uproar below pealed the bells; the morning sky rang with the noble summons to all brave men. Once more the ancient tower trembled with the mighty outcrash of the battle hymn.

With the last note she turned and looked down at him where he lay against the wall. He opened his glazing eyes and tried to smile at her.

"Bully," he whispered. "Could you recite— the words—to me—just so I could hear them on my way—West?"

She left the keyboard, came and dropped on her knees beside him; and closing her eyes to check the tears sang in a low, tremulous, girlish voice, De Lonlay's words, to the battle anthem of revolution.

"Bully," he sighed. And spoke no more on earth.

But the little mistress of the bells did not know his soul had passed.

And the French officer who came leaping up the stairs, pistol lifted, halted in astonishment to see a dead man lying beside a sack of bombs and a young girl on her knees beside him, weeping and tremblingly intoning "La Brabançonne."

CHAPTER XXI

A week later, toward noon, as usual, the two American muleteers, Smith and Glenn, sauntered over from their corral to the White Doe Tavern where, it being a meatless day, they ate largely of potato soup and of a tench, smoking hot.

The tench had been caught that morning off the back doorstep, which was an ancient and mossy slab of limestone let into the coping of the river wall.

Jean Courtray, the crippled inn-keeper, caught it. All that morning he had sat there in the sun on the river wall, half dozing, opening his dim eyes at intervals to gaze at his painted quill afloat among the water weeds of the little river Lesse. At intervals, too, he turned his head with that peculiar movement

of the old, and peered at his daughter, Maryette, and the Belgian gardener who were working among the potatoes in the garden.

And at last he had hooked his fish and the
emaciated young Belgian dropped his hoe and
came over and released it from the hook where
it lay flopping and quivering and glittering
among the wild grasses on the river bank. And
that was how Kid Glenn and Sticky Smith,
American muleteers on duty at Saint Lesse,
came to lunch on freshly caught tench at the
Inn of the White Doe.

After luncheon, agreeably satiated, they rose
from the table in the little dining room and
strolled out to the garden in the rear of the
inn, their Mexican spurs clanking. Maryette
heard them; they tipped their caps to her;
she acknowledged their salute gravely and continued to cultivate her garden with a hoe, the
blond, consumptive Belgian trundling a rickety
cultivator at her heels.

"Look, Stick," drawled Glenn. "Maryette's
got her decoration on."

From where they lounged by the river wall

they could see the cross of the Legion pinned to the girl's blouse.

Both muleteers had been present at the investment the day before, when a general officer arrived from Paris and the entire garrison of Sainte Lesse had been paraded—an impressive total of three dozen men—six gendarmes and a brigadier; one remount sub-lieutenant and twenty troopers; a veterinary, two white American muleteers, and five American negro hostlers from Baton Rouge.

The girl had nearly died of shyness during the ceremony, had endured the accolade with crimson cheeks, had stammered a whispered response to the congratulations of neighbors who had gathered to see the little bell-mistress of Sainte Lesse honoured by the country which she had served in the belfry of Nivelle.

As she came past Smith and Glenn, trailing her hoe, the latter now sufficiently proficient in French, said gaily:

"Have you heard from Jack again, Mamzelle Maryette?"

The girl blushed:

"I hear from Djack by every mail," she said, with all the transparent honesty that characterized her.

Smith grinned:

"Just like that! Well, tell him from me to quit fooling away his time in a hospital and come and get you or somebody is going to steal you."

The girl was very happy; she stood there in the September sunshine leaning on her hoe and gazing half shyly, half humorously down the river where a string of American mules was being watered.

Mellow Ethiopian laughter sounded from the distance as the Baton Rouge negroes exchanged pleasantries in limited French with a couple of gendarmes on the bank above them. And there, in the sunshine of the little garden by the river, war and death seemed very far away. Only at intervals the veering breeze brought to Sainte Lesse the immense vibration of the cannonade; only at intervals the high sky-clatter of an airplane reminded the village that the front was only a little north of Nivelle, and that what had been Nivelle was not so very far away.

"If you were *my* girl, Maryette," remarked Smith, "I'd die of worry in that hospital."

"*You* might have reason to, Monsieur," retorted the girl demurely. "But you see it's Djack who is convalescing, not you."

She had become accustomed to the ceaseless banter of Burley's two comrades—a banter entirely American, and which at first she was unable to understand. But now all things American, including accent and odd, perverted humour, had become very dear to her. The clink-clank of the muleteer's big spurs always set her heart beating; the sight of an arriving convoy from the Channel port thrilled her, and to her the trample of mules, the shouts of foreign negroes, the drawling, broken French spoken by the white muleteers made heavenly real to her the dream which love had so suddenly invaded, and into which, as suddenly, strode Death, clutching at Love.

She had beaten him off—she had—or God had—routed Death, driven him from the dream.

For it was a dream to her still, and she thought she could never be able to comprehend the magic reality of it, even when at last her man, "Djack," came back to prove the blessed miracle which held her in the magic of its thrall.

"Who's the guy with the wheelbarrow?" inquired Sticky Smith, rolling a cigarette.

"Karl, his name is," she answered; "—a Belgian refugee."

"He looks like a Hun to me," remarked Glenn, bluntly.

"He has his papers," said the girl.

Glenn shrugged.

"With his little pink eyes of a pig and his whitish hair and eyebrows—well, maybe they make 'em like that in Belgium."

"Papers," added Smith, "*can* be swiped."

The girl shook her head:

"He's an invalid student from Ypres. He looks quite ill, I think."

"He looks the lunger, all right. But Huns have it, too. What does he do—wander about town at will?"

"He works for us, monsieur. Your suspicions are harsh. Karl is quite harmless, poor boy."

"What does he do after hours?" demanded Sticky Smith, watching the manœuvres of the sickly blond youth and the wheelbarrow.

"Monsieur Smith, if you knew how innocent is his pastime!" she exclaimed, laughing. "He collects and studies moths and butterflies. Is there, if you please, a mania more harmless in the world? . . . And now I must return to my work, messieurs."

As the two muleteers strode clanking away toward the canal in the meadow, the blond youth turned his head and looked after them out of eyes which were naturally pale and small, and which, as he watched the two Americans, seemed to grow paler and smaller yet.

That afternoon old Courtray, swathed in a shawl, sat on the mossy doorstep and fished among the water weeds of the river. The sun was low; work in the garden had ended.

Maryette had gone up into her belfry to play the sunset hymn on the noble old carillon. Through the sunset sky the lovely bell-notes

floated far and wide, exquisitely chaste and
aloof as the high-showering ecstasy of a sky-
lark.

As always the little village looked upward
and listened, pausing in its humble duties as
long as their little bell-mistress remained in
her tower.

After the hymn she played "Myn hart is vol
verlangen" and "Het Lied der Vlamingen,"
and ended with the delicate, bewitching little
folk-song, "Myn Vryer," by Hasselt.

Then in the red glow of the setting sun the
girl laid aside her wooden gloves, rose from
the ancient keyboard, wound up the drum, and,
her duty done for the evening, came down out
of the tower among the transparent evening
shadows of the tree-lined village street.

The sun hung over Nivelle hills, which had
turned to amethyst. Sunbeams laced the little
river in a red net through which old Courtray's quill stemmed the ripples. He still
clutched his fishing pole, but his eyes were
closed, his chin resting on his chest.

Maryette came silently into the garden and
looked at her father—looked at the blond Karl

seated on the river wall beside the dozing angler. The blond youth had a box on his knees into which he was intently peering.

The girl came to the river wall and seated herself at her father's feet. The Belgian refugee student had already risen to attention, his heels together, but Maryette signed him to be seated again.

"What have you found now, Karl?" she inquired in a cautiously modulated voice.

"Ah, mademoiselle, fancy! I haff by chance with my cultivator among your potatoes already twenty pupæ of the magnificent moth, Sphinx Atropos, upturned! See! Regard them, mademoiselle! What lucky chance! What fortune for me, an entomologist, this wonderful sphinx moth to discover encased within its chrysalis!"

The girl smiled at his enthusiasm:

"But, Karl, those funny, smooth brown things which resemble little polished evergreen-cones are not rare in my garden. Often, when spading or hoeing among the potato vines, I uncover them."

"Mademoiselle, the caterpillar which makes this chrysalis feeds by night on the leaves of the potato, and, when ready to transform, burrows into the earth to become a chryalis or pupa, as we call it. That iss why mademoiselle has often disinterred the pupæ of this largest and strangest of our native sphinx-moths."

Maryette leaned over and looked into the wooden box, where lay the chrysalides.

"What kind of moth do they make?" she asked.

He blinked his small, pale eyes:

"The Death's Head," he said, complacently.

The girl recoiled involuntarily:

"Oh!" she exclaimed under her breath, "—*that* creature!"

For everywhere in France the great moth, with its strange and ominous markings, is perfectly well known. To the superstitious it is a creature of evil omen in its fulvous, black and lead-coloured livery of death. For the broad, furry thorax bears a skull, and the big, mousy body the yellow ribs of a skeleton.

Measuring often more than five inches across the expanded wings, its formidable size alone might be sufficient to inspire alarm, but in addition it possesses a horrid attribute unknown among other moths and butterflies; it can utter a cry—a tiny shrill, shuddering complaint. Small wonder, perhaps, that the peasant holds it in horror—this sleek, furry, powerfully winged creature marked with skull and bones, which whirrs through the night and comes thudding against the window, and shrieks horridly when touched by a human hand.

"So *that* is what turns into the Death's Head moth," said the girl in a low voice as though to herself. "I never knew it. I thought those things were legless cock-chafers when I dug them out of potato hills. Karl, why do you keep them?"

"Ah, mademoiselle! To study them. To breed from them the moth. The Death's Head is magnificent."

"God made it," admitted the girl with a faint shudder, "but I am afraid I could not love it. When do they hatch out?"

"It is time now. It is not like others of the sphinx family. Incubation requires but a few weeks. These are nearly ready to emerge, mademoiselle."

"Oh. And then what do they do?"

"They mate."

She was silent.

"The males seek the females," he said in his pedantic, monotonous voice. "And so ardent are the lovers that although there be no female moth within five, eight, perhaps ten miles, yet will her lover surely search through the night for her and find her."

Maryette shuddered again in spite of herself. The thought of this creature marked with the emblems of death and possessed of ardour, too, was distasteful.

"Amour macabre — what an unpleasant thought, Karl. I do not care for your Death's Head and for the history of their amours."

She turned and gently laid her head on her father's knees. The young man regarded her with a pallid sneer.

Addressing her back, still holding his boxful of pupæ on his bony knees, he said with the sneer quite audible in his voice:

"Your famous savant, Fabre, first inspired me to study the sex habits of the Death's Head."

She made no reply, her cheek resting on her father's knees.

"It was because of his wonderful experiments with the Great Peacock moth and with others of the genus that I have studied to acquaint myself concerning the amours of the Death's Head. *And I have discovered that he will find the female even if she be miles and miles away.*"

The man was grinning now in the dusk— grinning like a skull; but the girl's back was still turned and she merely found something in his voice not quite agreeable.

"I think," she said in a low, quiet voice, "that I have now heard sufficient about the Death's Head moth."

"Ah—have I offended mademoiselle? I ask a thousand pardons——"

Old Courtray awoke in the dusk.

"My quill, Maryette," he muttered, "—see if it floats yet?"

The girl bent over the water and strained her eyes. Her father tested the line with shaky hands. There was no fish on the hook.

"*Voyons!* The *asticot* also is gone. Some

robber fish has been nibbling!" exclaimed the girl cheerfully, reeling in the line. "Father, one cannot fish and doze at the same time."

"Eternal vigilance is the price of success—in peace as well as in war," said Karl, the student, as he aided Maryette to raise her father from the chair.

"Vigilance," repeated the girl. "Yes, always now in France. Because always the enemy is listening." . . . Her strong young arm around her father, she traversed the garden slowly toward the house. A pleasant odour came from the kitchen of the White Doe, where an old peasant woman was cooking.

CHAPTER XXII

THE SUSPECT

That night she wrote to her lover at the great hospital in the south, where he lay slowly growing well:

My Djack:

Today has been very beautiful, made so for me by my thoughts of you and by a warm September sun which makes for human happiness, too.

I am wearing my ribbon of the Legion. Ah, my Djack, it belongs more rightly to you, who would not let me go alone to Nivelle that dreadful day. Why do they not give you the cross? They must be very stupid in Paris.

All day my happy thoughts have been with you, my Djack. It all seems a blessed dream that we love each other. And I—oh, how could I have been so ignorant, so silly, not to know it sooner than I did!

I don't know; I thought it was friendship. And that was so wonderful to me that I never dreamed any other miracle possible!

Allons, my Djack. Come and instruct me quickly,

276

because my desire for further knowledge is very ardent.

The news? *Cher ami,* there is little. Always the far thunder beyond Nivelle in ruins; sometimes a battle-plane high in the blue; a convoy of your beloved mules arriving from the coast; nothing more exciting.

Monsieur Smeet and Monsieur Glenn inquire always concerning you. They are brave and kind; their odd jests amuse me.

My father caught a tench in the Lesse this morning.

My gardener, Karl, collected many unpleasant creatures while hoeing our potatoes. Poor lad, he seems unhealthy. I am glad I could offer him employment.

My Djack, there could not possibly be any mistake about him, could there? His papers are en règle. He is what he pretends, a Belgian student from Ypres in distress and ill health, is he not?

But how can you answer me, you who lie there all alone in a hospital at Nice? Also, I am ashamed of myself for doubting the unfortunate young man. I am too happy to doubt anybody, perhaps.

And so good night, my Djack. Sleep sweetly, guarded by powerful angels.

Thy devoted,
MARYETTE.

She had been writing in the deserted café. Now she took a candle and went slowly up-

stairs. On the white plaster wall of her bedroom was a Death's Head moth.

The girl, startled for an instant, stood still;
an unfeigned shiver of displeasure passed over
her. Not that the Death's Head was an unfamiliar or terrifying sight to her; in late
summer she usually saw one or two which had
flown through some lighted window.

But it was the amorous history of this creature which the student Karl had related that
now repelled her. This night creature with
the skull on its neck, once scarcely noticed, had
now become a trifle repulsive.

She went nearer, lifting the lighted candle.
The thing crouched there with slanted wings.
It was newly hatched, its sleek body still wet
with the humors of incubation—wet as a
soaked mouse. Its abdomen, too, seemed enormous, all swelled and distended with unfertil-
ized eggs. No, there could be no question concerning the sex of the thing; this was a female,
and her tumefied body was almost bursting
with eggs.

In startling design the yellow skull stood
out; the ribs of the skeleton. Two tiny, fiery

eyes glimmered at the base of the antennæ—
two minute jewelled sparks of glowing, lambent
fire. They seemed to be watching her, mali-
ciously askance.

The very horrid part of it was that, if
touched, the creature would cry out. The girl
knew this, hesitated, looked at the open window
through which it must have crawled, and sat
down on her bed to consider the situation.

"After all," she said to herself resolutely.
"God made it. It is harmless. If God thought
fit to paint one of his lesser creatures like a
skeleton, perhaps it was to remind us that
life is brief and that we should lose no time
to live it nobly in His sight. . . . I think that
perhaps explains it."

However, she did not undress.

"I am quite foolish to be afraid of this
poor moth. I repeat that I am foolish. *Allez*
—I am *not* afraid. I am no longer afraid. I
—I admire this handiwork of God."

She sat looking at the creature, her hands
lying clasped in her lap.

"It's a very odd thing," she said to herself,
"that a lover can find this creature even if he

be miles and miles away. . . . Maybe he's on his way now——"

Instinctively she sprang up and closed her bedroom window.

"No," she said, looking severely at the motionless moth, "you shall have no visitors in my room. You may remain here; I shall not disturb you; and tomorrow you will go away of your own accord. But I cannot permit you to receive company——"

A heavy fall on the floor above checked her. Breathless, listening, she crept to her door.

"Karl!" she called.

Listening again, she could hear distant and vaguely dreadful sounds from the gardener-student's room above.

She was frightened but she went up. The youth had had a bad hemorrhage. She sat beside him late into the night. After his breathing grew quieter, sitting there in silence she could hear odd sounds, rustling, squeaking sounds from the box of Death's Head chrysalids on the night table beside his bed.

The pupæ of the Death's Head were making merry in anticipation of the rapidly approach-

ing change—the Great Adventure of their lives
—the coming metamorphosis.

The youth lay asleep now. As she extinguished the candle and stole from the room, all
the pupæ of the Death's Head began to squeak
in the darkness.

The student-gardener could do no more
work for the present. He lay propped up in
bed, pasty, scarlet lipped, and he seemed bald
and lidless, so colourless were hair and eyelashes.

"Can I do anything for you, Karl?" asked
Maryette, coming in for a moment as usual in
the intervals of her many duties.

"The ink, if you would be so condescending
—and a pen," he said, watching her out of
hollow, sallow eyes of watery blue.

She fetched both from the café.

She came again in another hour, knocking
at his door, but he said rather sharply that
he wished to sleep.

Scarcely noticing the querulous tone, she
departed. She had much to do besides her duties in the belfry. Her father was an invalid

who required constant care; there was only one servant, an old peasant woman who cooked. The Government required her father to keep open the White Doe Tavern, and there was always a little business from the scanty garrison of Sainte Lesse, always a few meals to get, a few drinks to serve, and nobody now to do it except herself.

Then, in the belfry she had duties other than playing, than practice. Always at night the clock-drum was to be wound.

She had no assistant. The town maintained none, and her salary as Mistress of the Bells of Sainte Lesse did not permit her to engage anybody to help her.

So she oiled and wound all the machinery herself, adjusted and cared for the clock, swept the keyboard clean, inspected and looked after the wires leading to the tiers of bells overhead.

Then there was work to do in the garden— a few minutes snatched between other duties. And when night arrived at last she was rather tired—quite weary on this night in particular, having managed to fulfill all the duties of the sick youth as well as her own.

The night was warm and fragrant. She sat in the dark at her open window for a while, looking out into the north where, along the horizon, heat lightning seemed to play. But it was only the reflected flashes of the guns. When the wind was right, she could hear them.

She had even managed to write to her lover. Now, seated beside the open window, she was thinking of him. A dreamy, happy lethargy possessed her; she was on the first delicate verge of slumber, so close to it that all earthly sounds were dying out in her ears. Then, suddenly, she was awake, listening.

A window had been opened in the room overhead.

She went to the stars and called:

"Karl!"

"What?" came the impatient reply.

"Are you ill?"

"No. N-no, I thank you—" His voice became urbane with an apparent effort. "Thank you for inquiring——"

"I heard your window open—" she said.

"Thank you. I am quite well. The air is mild and grateful. . . . I thank mademoiselle for her solicitude."

She returned to her room and lighted her candle. On the white plaster wall sat the Death's Head moth.

She had not been in her room all day. She was astonished that the moth had not left.

"Shall I have to put you out?" she thought dubiously. "Really, I can not keep my window closed for fear of visitors for you, Madam Death! I certainly shall be obliged to put you out."

So she found a sheet of paper and a large glass tumbler. Over the moth she placed the tumbler, then slipped the sheet of paper under the glass between moth and wall.

The thing cried and cried, beating at the glass with wings as powerful as a bird's, and the girl, startled and slightly repelled, placed the moth on her night table, imprisoned under the tumbler.

For a while it fluttered and flapped and cried out in its strange, uncanny way, then settled on the sheet of paper, quivering its wings, both eyes like living coals.

Seated on the bedside, Maryette looked at it, schooling herself to think of it kindly as one of God's creatures before she released it at her open window.

And, as she sat there, something came whizzing into the room through her window, circled around her at terrific speed with a humming, whispering whirr, then dropped with a solid thud on the night table beside the imprisoned female moth.

It was the first suitor arrived from outer darkness—a big, powerful Death's Head moth with eyes aglow, the yellow skull displayed in startling contrast on his velvet-black body.

The girl watched him, fascinated. He scrambled over to the tumbler, tested it with heavy antennæ; then, ardent and impatient, beat against the glass with muscular wings that clattered in the silence.

But it was not the amorous fury of the creature striking the tumbler with resounding wings, not the glowing eyes, the strong, clawed feet, the Death's Head staring from its funereal black thorax that held the girl's attention. It was something else; something entirely different riveted her eyes on the creature.

For the cigar-shaped body, instead of bearing the naked ribs of a skeleton, was snow white.

And now she began to understand. Somebody had already caught the moth, had wrapped around its body a cylinder of white tissue paper—tied it on with a fine, white silk thread.

The moth was very still now, exploring the interstices between tumbler and table with heavy, pectinated antennæ.

Cautiously Maryette bent forward and dropped both hands on the moth.

Instantly the creature cried out horribly; it was like a mouse between her shrinking fingers; but she slipped the cylinder of tissue paper from its abdomen and released it with a shiver; and it darted and whizzed around the room, gyrating in whistling circles around her head until, unnerved, she struck at it again and again with empty hands, following, driving it toward the open window, out of which it suddenly darted.

But now there was another Death's Head in the room, a burly, headlong, infatuated male which drove headlong at the tumbler and clung to it, slipping, sliding, filling the room with a feathery tattoo of wings.

It, also, had a snow-white body; and before she had seized the squeaking thing and had slipped the tissue wrapper from its body, another Death's Head whirred through the window; then another, then two; then others. The room swarmed; they were crawling all over the tumbler, the table, the bed. The room was filled with the soft, velvety roar of whirring wings beating on wall and ceiling and against the tumbler where Madam Death sat imprisoned, quivering her wings, her eyes two molten rubies, and the ghastly skull staring from her back.

How Maryette ever brought herself to do it; how she did it at last, she had no very clear idea. The touch of the slippery, mousy bodies was fearsomely repugnant to her; the very sight of the great, skull-bearing things began to sicken her physically. A dreadful, almost impalpable floss from their handled wings and bodies smeared her hands; the place vibrated with their tiny goblin cries.

Somehow she managed to strip them of the tissue cylinders, drive them from where they crawled on ceiling, wall and sill into whistling flight. Amid a whirlwind of wings she fought them toward the open window; whizzing, flitting, circling they sped in widening spirals to escape her blows, where she stood half blinded in the vortex of the ghostly maelstrom.

One by one they darted through the open window out into the night; and when the last spectral streak of grey had sped into outer darkness the girl slammed the windowpanes shut and leaned against the sill enervated, exhausted, revolted.

The room was misty with the microscopic dust from the creatures' wings; on her palms and fingers were black stains and stains of livid orange; and across wall and ceiling streaks and smudges of rusty colour.

She was still trembling when she washed the smears from her hands. Her fingers were still unsteady as she smoothed out each tiny sheet of tissue paper and laid it on her night table. Then, seated on the bed's edge beside the lighted candle, she began to read the messages written in ink on these frail, translucent tissue missives.

Every bit of tissue bore a message; the writing was microscopic, the script German, the language Flemish. Slowly, with infinite pains, the little bell-mistress of Sainte Lesse translated to herself each message as she deciphered it.

She was trembling more than ever when she finished. Every trace of colour had fled from her cheeks.

Then, as she sat there, struggling to keep her mind clear of the horror of the thing, striving to understand what was to be done, there came upon her window pane a sudden muffled drumming sound, and her frightened gaze fell upon a Death's Head moth outside, its eyes like coals, its misty wings beating furiously for admittance. And around its body was tied a cylinder of white tissue.

But the girl needed no more evidence. The

wretched youth in the room overhead had already sealed his own doom with any one of these tissue cylinders. Better for him if the hemorrhage had slain him. Now a firing squad must do that much for him.

Yet, even still, the girl hesitated, almost incredulous, trying to comprehend the monstrous grotesquerie of the abominable plot.

Intuition pointed to the truth; logic proved it; somewhere in the German trenches a comrade of this spy was awaiting these messages with a caged Death's Head female as the bait —a living loadstone wearing the terrific emblems of death—an unfailing magnet to draw the skull-bearing messengers for miles—had it not been that a *nearer magnet deflected them in their flight!*

That was it! That was what the miserable youth upstairs had not counted on. Chance had ruined him; destiny had sent Madam Death into the room below him to draw, with her macabre charms, every ardent winged messenger which he liberated from his bedroom window.

The subtle effluvia permeating the night air

for miles around might have guided these messengers into the German trenches had not a nearer and more imperious perfume annihilated it. Headlong, amorous, impatient they had whirled toward the embraces of Madam Death; the nearer and more powerful perfume had drawn the half-maddened, half-drugged messengers. The spy in the room upstairs, like many Germans, had reasoned wrongly on sound premises. His logic had broken down, not his amazing scientific foundation. His theory was correct; his application stupid.

And now this young man was about to die. Maryette understood that. She comprehended that his death was necessary; that it was the unavoidable sequence of what he had attempted to do. Trapped rats must be drowned; vermin exterminated by easiest and quickest methods; spies who betray one's native land pass naturally the same route.

But this thing, this grotesque, incredible, terrible attempt to engraft treachery on one of nature's most amazing laws—this secret, cunning Teutonic reasoning, this scientific scoundrelism, this criminal enterprise based on pa-

tient, plodding and German efficiency, still bewildered the girl.

And yet she vaguely realized how science had
been already prostituted to Prussian malig-
nancy and fury; she had heard of flame jets,
of tear-bombs, of bombs containing deadly
germs; she herself had beheld the poison gas
rolling back into the trenches at Nivelle under
the town tower. Dimly she began to understand that the Hun, in his cunning savagery,
had tricked, betrayed and polluted civilization
itself into lending him her own secrets with
which she was ultimately to be destroyed.

The very process of human thinking had
been imitated by these monkeys of Europe—
apes with the ferocity of hogs—and no souls,
none—nothing to lift them inside the pale
where dwells the human race.

There came a rapping on the café door.
The girl rose wearily; an immense weight
seemed to crush her shoulders so that her
knees had become unsteady.

She opened the café door; it was Sticky
Smith, come for his nightcap before turning in.

"The man upstairs is a German spy," she said listlessly. "Had you not better go over and get a gendarme?"

"Who's a spy? That Dutch shrimp you had in your garden?"

"Yes."

"Where is he?" demanded the muleteer with an oath.

She placed her lighted candle on the bar.

"Wait," she said. "Read these first—we must be quite certain about what we do."

She laid the squares of tissue paper out on the bar.

"Do you read Flemish?" she whispered.

"No, ma'am——"

"Then I will translate into French for you. And first of all I must tell you how I came to possess these little letters written upon tissue. Please listen attentively."

He rested his palm on the butt of his dangling automatic.

"Go on," he said.

She told him the circumstances.

As she commenced to translate the tissue paper messages in a low, tremulous voice, the sound of a door being closed and locked in the room overhead silenced her.

The next instant she had stepped out to the stairs and called:

"Karl!"

There was no reply. Smith came out to the stair-well and listened.

"It is his custom," she whispered, "to lock his door before retiring. That is what we heard."

"Call again."

"He can't hear me. He is in bed."

"Call, all the same."

"Karl!" she cried out in an unsteady voice.

CHAPTER XXIII

MADAM DEATH

There was no reply, because the young man was hanging out over his window sill in the darkness trying to switch away, from her closed window below, the big, clattering Death's Head moth which obstinately and persistently fluttered there.

What possessed the moth to continue battering its wings at the window of the room below? Had the other moths which he released done so, too? They had darted out of his room into the night, each garnished with a tissue robe. He supposed they had flown north; he had not looked out to see.

What had gone wrong with this moth, then?

He took his emaciated blond head between his bony fingers and pondered, probing for reason with German thoroughness—that cele-

295

brated thoroughness which is invariably rid-
dled with flaws.

Of all contingencies he had thought—or so
it seemed to him. He could not recollect any
precaution neglected. He had come to Sainte
Lesse for a clearly defined object and to make
certain reports concerning matters of interest
to the German military authorities north of
Nivelle.

The idea, inspired by the experiments of
Henri Fabre, was original with him. Patiently, during the previous year, he had worked
it out—had proved his theory by a series of
experiments with moths of this species.

He had arranged with his staff comrade,
Dr. Glück, for a forced hatching of the pupæ
which the latter had patiently bred from the
enormous green and violet-banded caterpillars.

At least one female Death's Head must be
ready, caged in the trenches beyond Nivelle.
Hundreds of pupæ could not have died. Where,
then, was his error—if, indeed, he had made
any?

Leaning from the window, he looked down

at the frantic moth, perplexed, a little uneasy now.

"Swine!" he muttered. "What, then, ails you that you do not fly to the mistress awaiting you over yonder?"

He could see the cylinder of white tissue shining on the creature's body, where it fluttered against the pane, illuminated by the rays of the candle from within the young girl's room.

Could it be possible that the candle-light was proving the greater attraction?

Even as the possibility entered his mind, he saw another Death's Head dart at the window below and join the first one. But this new-comer wore no tissue jacket.

Then, out of the darkness the Death's Heads began to come to the window below, swarms of them, startling him with the racket of their wings.

From where did they arrive? They could not be the moths he liberated. But. . . . *Were they?* Had some accident robbed their bodies of the tissue missives? Had they blundered into somebody's room and been robbed?

Mystified, uneasy, he hung over his window sill, staring with sickening eyes at the winged tumult below.

With patient, plodding logic he began to seek for the solution. What attracted these moths to the room below? Was it the candlelight? That alone could not be sufficient—could not contend with the more imperious attraction, the subtle effluvia stealing out of the north and appealing to the ruling passion which animated the frantic winged things below him.

Patiently, methodically in his mind he probed about for some clue to the solution. The ruling passion animating the feathery whirlwind below was the necessity for mating and perpetuating the species.

That was the dominant passion; the lure of candle-light a secondary attraction. . . . Then, if this were so—and it had been proven to be a fact—then—then—*what* was in that young girl's bedroom just below him?

Even as the question flashed in his mind he left the window, went to his door, listened, noiselessly unlocked it.

A low murmur of voices came from the café.

He drew off both shoes, descended the stairs on the flat pads of his large, bony feet, listening all the while.

Candle-light streamed out into the corridor from her open bedroom door; and he crept to the sill and peered in, searching the place with small, pale eyes.

At first he noticed nothing to interest him, then, all in an instant, his gaze fell upon Madam Death under her prison of glass.

There she sat, her great bulging abdomen distended with eggs, her lambent eyes shining with the terrible passion of anticipation. For one thing only she had been created. That accomplished she died. And there she crouched awaiting the fulfillment of her life's cycle with the blazing eyes of a demon.

From the café below came the cautious murmur of voices. The young man already knew what they were whispering about; or, if he did not know he no longer cared.

The patches of bright colour in his sunken

cheeks had died out in an ashen pallor. As far as he was concerned the world was now ended. And he knew it.

He went into the bedroom and sat down on the bed's edge. His little, pale eyes wandered about the white room; the murmur of voices below was audible all the while.

After a few moments' patient waiting, his gaze rested again on Madam Death, squatting there with wings sloped, and the skull and bones staring at him from her head and distended abdomen.

After all there was an odd resemblance between himself and Madam Death. He had been born to fulfill one function, it appeared. So had she. And now, in his case as in hers, death was immediately to follow. This was sentiment, not science—the blind lobe of the German brain balancing grotesquely the reasoning lobe.

The voices below had ceased. Presently he heard a cautious step on the stair.

He had a little pill-box in his pocket. Methodically, without haste, he drew it out, chose one white pellet, and, holding it between his bony thumb and forefinger, listened.

Yes, somebody was coming up the stairs, very careful to make no sound.

Well—there were various ways for a Death's Head Hussar to die for his War Lord. All were equally laudable. God—the God of Germany—the celestial friend and comrade of his War Lord—would presently correct him if he was transgressing military discipline or the etiquette of Kultur. As for the levelled rifles of the execution squad, he preferred another way. . . . *This* way! . . .

His eyes were already glazing when the burly form of Sticky Smith filled the doorway.

He looked down at Madam Death under the tumbler beside him, then lifted his head and gazed at Smith with blinded eyes.

"Swine!" he said complacently, swaying gently forward and striking the floor with his face.

CHAPTER XXIV

BUBBLES

An east wind was very likely to bring gas to the trenches north of the Sainte Lesse salient. A north wind, according to season, brought snow or rain or fog upon British, French, Belgian and Boche alike. Winds of the south carried distant exhalations from orchards and green fields into the pitted waste of ashes where that monstrous desolation stretched away beneath a thundering iron rain which beat all day, all night upon the dead flesh of the world.

But the west wind was the vital wind, flowing melodiously through the trees—a clean, aromatic, refreshing wind, filling the sickened world with life again.

Sometimes, too, it brought the pleasant music of the bells into far-away trenches, when the little bell-mistress of Sainte Lesse played the carillon. And when her friend, the great bell, Bayard, spoke through the resounding sky of France to a million men-at-arms in blue and steel, who were steadily forging hell's manacles for the uncaged Hun, the loyal western wind carried far beyond the trenches an ominous iron vibration that meant doom for the Beast.

And the Beast heard, leering skyward out of pale pig-eyes, but did not comprehend.

At the base corral down in the meadow, mules had been scarce recently, because a transport had been torpedoed. But the next transport from New Orleans escaped; the dusty column had arrived at Sainte Lesse from the Channel port, convoyed by American muleteers, as usual; new mules, new negroes, new Yankee faces invaded the town once more.

However, it signified little to the youthful mistress - of - the - bells, Maryette Courtray, called "Carillonnette," for her Yankee lover still lay in his distant hospital—her muleteer, "Djack." So mules might bray, and negroes fill the Sainte Lesse meadows with their shouting laughter; and the lank, hawk-nosed Yankee muleteers might saunter clanking into the White Doe in search of meat or drink or tobacco, or a glimpse of the pretty bell-mistress, for all it meant to her.

Her Djack lived; that was what occupied her mind; other men were merely men—even his comrades, Sticky Smith and Kid Glenn, assumed individuality to distinguish them from other men only because they were Djack's friends. And as for all other muleteers, they seemed to her as alike as Chinamen, leaving upon her young mind a general impression of long, thin legs and necks and the keen eyes of hunting falcons.

She had washing to do that morning. Very early she climbed up into the ancient belfry, wound the drum so that the bells would play a few bars at the quarters and before each hour struck; and also in order that the carillon might ring mechanically at noon in case she had not returned to take her place at the keyboard with her wooden gloves.

There was a light west wind rippling through

the tree tops; and everywhere sunshine lay brilliant on pasture and meadow under the purest of cobalt skies.

In the garden her crippled father, swathed in shawls, dozed in his deep chair beside the river-wall, waking now and then to watch the quill on his long bamboo fish-pole, stemming the sparkling current of the little river Lesse.

Sticky Smith, off duty and having filled himself to repletion with café-au-lait at the inn, volunteered to act as nurse, attendant, remover of fish and baiter of hook, while Maryette was absent at the stone-rimmed pool where the washing of all Sainte Lesse laundry had been accomplished for hundreds of years.

"You promise not to go away?" she cautioned him in the simple, first-aid French she employed in speaking to him, and pausing with both arms raised to balance the loaded clothes-basket on her head.

"Wee—wee!" he assured her with dignity. "Je fume mong peep! Je regard le vieux pêcher. Voo poovay allay, Mademoiselle Maryette."

She hesitated, then removed the basket from her head and set it on the grass.

"You are very kind, Monsieur Steek-Smeet. I shall wash your underwear the very first garments I take out of my basket. Thank you a thousand times." She bent over with sweet solicitude and pressed her lips to her father's withered cheek:

"Au revoir, my father *chéri*. An hour or two at the meadow-*lavoir* and I shall return to find thee. *Bonne chance, mon père!* Thou shalt surely catch a large and beautiful fish for luncheon before I return with my wash."

She swung the basket of wash to her head again without effort, and went her way, following the deeply trodden sheep-path behind the White Doe Inn.

The path wound down through a sloping pasture, across a footbridge spanning an arm of the Lesse which washed the base of the garden wall, then ascended a gentle aclivity among hazel thicket and tall sycamores, becoming for a little distance a shaded wood-path where thrushes sang ceaselessly in the sun-flecked undergrowth.

But at the eastern edge of the copse the little hill fell away into an open, sunny meadow, fragrant with wild-flowers and clover, through which a rivulet ran deep and cold between grassy banks.

It supplied the drinking water of Sainte Lesse; and a branch of it poured bubbling into the stone-rimmed *lavoir* where generations of Sainte Lesse maids had scrubbed the linen of the community, kneeling there amid wild flowers and fluttering butterflies in the shade of three tall elms.

There was nobody at the pool; Maryette saw that as she came out of the hazel copse through the meadow. And very soon she was on her knees at the clear pool's edge, bare of arm and throat and bosom, her blue wool skirts trussed up, and elbow deep in snowy suds.

Overhead the sky was a quivering, royal blue; the earth shimmered in its bath of sunshine; the west wind blowing carried away eastward the reverberations of the distant cannonade, so that not even the vibration of the concussions disturbed Sainte Lesse.

A bullfinch was piping lustily in a young tree as she began her task; a blackbird answered from somewhere among the hawthorns with a bewildering series of complicated trills.

As the little mistress-of-the-bells scrubbed and beat the clothes with her paddle, and rinsed and wrung them and soaped them afresh, she sang softly under her breath, to an ancient air of her *pays*, words that she improvised to fit it—*vrai chanson de laveuse:*

> "A blackbird whistles
>   I love!
> Over the thistles
> Butterflies hover,
> Each with her lover
>   In love.
> Blue Demoiselles that glisten,
>   Listen, I love!
> Wind of the west, oh, listen,
>   I am in love!
> Sing my song, ye little gold bees!
> Opal bubbles around my knees
> All afloat in the soap-sud broth,
> Whisper it low to the snowy froth;
> And Thou who rulest the skies above,
> Mary, adored—I love—I love!"

Slap-slap! went her paddle; the sud-spume flew like shreds of cotton; iridescent foam set with bubbles swirled in the stone-edged basin, constantly swept away down stream by the current, constantly renewed as she soaped and scrubbed, kneeling there in the meadow grass above the pool.

The blackbird came quite near to watch her; the bullfinch, attracted by her childish voice as she sang the song she was making, whistled bold response, silent only when the echoing slap of the paddle startled him where he sat on the trembling tip of an aspen.

Blue dragon flies drifted on glimmering wings; she put them into her song; the meadow was gay with butterflies' painted wings; she sang about them, too. Cloud and azure sky, tree tops and clover, the tiny rivulet dancing through deep grasses, the wind furrowing the fields, all these she put into her *chansonnette de laveuse.* And always in the clear glass of the stream she seemed to see the smiling face of her friend, Djack—her lover who had opened her eyes of a child to all things beautiful in the world.

Once or twice, from very far away, she fancied she heard the distant singing of the negro muleteers sunning themselves down by the corral. She heard, at quarter-hour intervals, her bells melodiously recording time as it sped by; then there were intervals of that sweet stillness which is but a composite harmony of summer—the murmur of insects, the whisper of leaves and water, capricious seconds of intense silence, then the hushed voice of life exquisitely audible again.

War, wickedness, the rage and cruelty of the Beast—all the vile and filthy ferocity of the ferocious Swine of the North became to her as unreal as a tragic legend half-forgotten. And death seemed very far away.

Her washing was done; the wet clothing piled in her basket. Perspiration powdered her forehead and delicate little nose.

Hot, flushed, breathing deeply and irregularly from her efforts under a vertical sun, she stood erect, loosening the blouse over her bosom to the breeze and pushing back the clustering masses of hair above her brow.

The water laughed up at her, invitingly; the last floating castle of white foam swept past her feet down stream. On the impulse of the moment she unlaced her blue wool skirt, dropped it around her feet, stepped from it; unbuckled both garters, stripped slippers and stockings from her feet, and waded out into the pool.

The fresh, delicious coolness of the water thrilled and encouraged her to further adventure; she twisted up her splendid hair, bound it with her blue kerchief, flung blouse and chemisette from her, and gave herself to the sparkling stream with a sigh of ecstasy.

Alders swept the eastern edges of the current where the rivulet widened beyond the basin and ran south along the meadow's edge to the Wood of Sainte Lesse—a cool, unruffled flow, breast deep, floored with sand as soft as silver velvet.

She waded, floated, swam a little, or, erect, roamed leisurely along the alder fringe, exploring the dim green haunts of frog and water-hen, stoat and bécassine—a slim, wet dryad, gliding silently through sun and dappled shadow.

Where the stream comes to Sainte Lesse

Wood, there is a hill set thick with hazel and clumps of fern, haunted by one roe-deer and numerous rabbits and pheasants.

She was close to its base, now, gliding through the shade like some lithe creature of the forest; making no sound save where the current curled around her supple body in twisted necklaces of liquid light.

Then, as she stood, peering cautiously through tangled branches for a glimpse of the little roe-deer, she heard a curious sound up on the hill—an inexplicable sound like metal striking stone.

She stood as though frozen; clink, clink came the distant sound. Then all was still. But presently she saw a scared cock-pheasant, crouching low with flattened neck outstretched, run like a huge rat through the hazel growth, out across the meadow.

She remained motionless, scarcely daring to draw her breath. Somebody had passed over the hill—if, indeed, he or she had actually continued on their mysterious way. Had they? But finally the intense quiet reassured her, and she concluded that whoever had made that metallic sound had continued on toward Sainte Lesse Wood.

She had taken with her a cake of soap. Now, here in the green shade, she made her ablutions, soaping herself from head to foot, turning her head leisurely from time to time to survey her leafy environment, or watch the flight of some tiny woodland bird, or study with pretty and speculative eyes the soap-suds swirling in a dimpled whirlpool around her thighs.

The bubbles fascinated her; she played with them, capriciously, touching one here, one there, with tentative finger to see them explode in a tiny rainbow shower.

Finally she chose a hollow stem from among a cluster of scented rushes, cleared it with a vigorous breath, soaped one end, and, touching it to the water, blew from it a prodigious bubble, all swimming with gold and purple hues.

Into the air she tossed it, from the end of the hollow reed; the breeze caught it and wafted it upward until it burst.

Then a strange thing happened! Before her

upturned eyes another bubble slowly arose from a clump of aspens out of the hazel thickets on the hill—a big, pearl-tinted, translucent bubble, as large as a melon. Upward it floated, slowly ascending to the tree-tops. There the wind caught it, drove it east, but it still mounted skyward, higher, higher, sailing always eastward, until it dwindled to the size of a thistledown and faded away in mid-air.

Astounded, the little mistress-of-the-bells stood motionless, waist deep in the stream, lips parted, eyes straining to pierce the dazzling ether above.

And then, before her incredulous gaze, another pearl-tinted, translucent bubble slowly floated upward from the thicket near the aspens, mounted until the breeze struck it, then soared away skyward and melted like a snowflake into the east.

Moving as stealthily as some sinuous creature of the water-weeds, the girl stole forward, threading her way among the rushes, gliding, twisting around tussock and alder, creeping along fern-set banks, her eyes ever focused on the clump of aspens quivering against the sky above the hazel.

She could see nobody, hear not a sound from the thicket on the little hill. But another bubble rose above the aspens as she looked.

Naked, she dared not advance into the woods —scarcely dared linger where she was, yet found enough courage to creep out on a carpet of moss and lie flat under a young fir, listening and watching.

No more bubbles rose above the aspens; there was not a sound, not a movement in the hazel.

For an hour or more she lay there; then, with infinite caution, she slipped back into the stream, waded across, crept into the meadow, and sped like a scared fawn along the bank until she stood panting by the stone-rimmed pool again.

Sun and wind had dried her skin; she dressed rapidly, swung her basket to her head, and started swiftly for Sainte Lesse.

Before she came in sight of the White Doe Tavern, she could hear the negro muleteers singing down by the corral.

Sticky Smith still squatted in the garden by the river-wall, smoking his pipe. Her father lay asleep in his chair, his wrinkled hands still clasping the fishing pole, the warm breeze blowing his white hair at the temples.

She disposed of the wash; then she and Sticky Smith gently aroused the crippled bell-master and aided him into the house.

The old peasant woman who cooked for the inn had soup ready. The noonday meal in Sainte Lesse had become an extremely simple affair.

"Monsieur Steek," said the girl carelessly, "did you ever, as a child, fly toy balloons?"

"Sure, Maryette. A old Eyetalian wop used to come 'round town selling them. He had a stick with about a hundred little balloons tied to it—red, blue, green, yellow—all kinds and colours. Whenever I had the price I bought one."

"Did it fly?"

"Yes. The gas in it wasn't much good unless you got a fresh one."

"Would it fly high?"

"Sure. Sky-high. I've seen 'em go clean out of sight when you got a fresh one."

"Nobody uses them here, do they?"

"Here? No, it wouldn't be allowed. A spy could send a message by one of those toy balloons."

"Oh," nodded Maryette thoughtfully.

Smith shook his head:

"No, children wouldn't be permitted to play with them things now, Maryette."

"Then there are not any toy balloons to be had here in Sainte Lesse?"

"I rather guess not! Farther north there are."

"Where?"

"The artillery uses them."

"How?"

"I don't know. The balloon and flying service use 'em, too. I've seen officers send them up. Probably it is to find out about upper air-currents."

"*Our* flying service?"

"Yes, ma'am."

"*Ballons d'essai*," she nodded carelessly.

But she was not yet entirely convinced regarding the theory she was pondering.

After lunch she continued to be very busy in the laundry for a time, but the memory of those three little balloons above the aspens troubled her.

Smith had gone on duty at the corral; Kid Glenn sauntered clanking into the bar and was there regaled with a *bock* and a *tranche*.

"Monsieur Keed," said Maryette, "are any of our airmen in Sainte Lesse today?"

Glenn drained his glass and smacked his lips:

"No, ma'am," he said.

"No balloonists, either?"

"I don't guess so, Maryette. We've got the Boche flyers scared stiff. They don't come over our first lines any more, and our own people are out yonder."

"Keed," she said, winningly sweet, "do you, in fact, love me a little—for Djack's sake?"

"Yes'm."

"I borrow of you that automatic pistol. Yes?" She smiled at him engagingly.

"Sure. Anything you want! What's the trouble, Maryette?"

She shrugged her pretty shoulders:

"Nothing. It just came into my cowardly head that the path to the *lavoir* is lonely at sundown. And there are new muleteers in Sainte Lesse. And I must wash my clothes."

"I reckon," he said gravely, unbuckling his weapon-filled holster and quietly strapping it around her shoulder with its pocketed belt of clips.

"You will not require it this afternoon?" she asked.

"No fear. You won't either. Them mule-whacking coons is white."

She understood.

"Some men who seem whitest are blacker than any negro," she remarked. *"Eh, bien!* I thank you, Keed, *mon ami*, for your complaisance. You are very amiable to submit to the whim of a silly girl who suddenly becomes afraid of her own shadow."

Glenn grinned and glanced significantly at the cross dangling from her bosom:

"Sure," he said, "your government decorates

cowards. That's why it gave you the Legion."

She blushed but looked up at him seriously:

"Keed, if I flew a little toy balloon in the air, where would the west wind carry it?"

"Into the Boche trenches," he replied, much interested in the idea. "If you've got one, we'll paint 'To hell with Willie' on it and set it afloat! But we'll have to get permission from the gendarmes first."

She said, smiling:

"I'm sorry, but I haven't any toy balloons."

She picked up her basket with its new load of soiled linen, swung it gracefully to her head, ignoring his offered assistance, gave him a beguiling glance, and went away along the sheep-path.

Once more she followed the deep-trodden and ancient trail through copse and pasture and over the stream down into the meadow, where the west wind furrowed the wild-flowers and the early afternoon sun fell hot.

She set her clothes to soak, laid paddle and soap beside them, then, straightening up, remained erect on her knees, her intent gaze fixed on the distant clump of aspens, delicate as mist above the hazel copse on the little hill beyond.

It was a whole hour before her eyes caught the high glimmer of a tiny balloon. Only for a moment was it visible at that distance, then it became merged in the dazzling blue above the woods.

She waited. At last she concluded that there were to be no more balloons. Then a sudden fear assailed her lest she had waited too long to investigate; and she sprang to her feet, hurried over the single plank used as a footbridge, and sped down through the alders.

Here and there a pheasant ran headlong across her path; a rabbit or two scuttled through the ferns. Nearing the hazel copse she slackened speed and advanced with caution, scanning the thicket ahead.

Suddenly, on the ground in front of her, she caught sight of a small iron cylinder. Evidently it had rolled down there from the slope above.

Very gingerly she approached and picked it up. It was not very heavy, not too big for her skirt pocket.

As she slipped it into the pocket of her blue woolen peasant-skirt, her quick eye caught a movement among the hazel bushes on the hillside to her right. She sank to the ground and lay huddled there.

CHAPTER XXV.

KAMERAD

Down the slope, through the thicket, came a man. She could see his legs only. He wore dust-coloured breeches and tan puttees, like Sticky Smith's and Kid Glenn's, only he wore no big, clanking Mexican spurs.

The man passed in front of her, his burly body barely visible through the leaves, but not his features.

She rose, turned, ran over the moss, hurried through the ferns of the warren, retracing her steps, and arrived breathless at the *lavoir*. And scarcely had she dropped to her knees and seized soap and paddle, than a squat, bronzed, powerfully built young man appeared on the opposite bank of the stream, stepping briskly out of the bushes.

He did not notice her at first. He looked

about for a place to jump, found one, leaped safely across, and came on at a swinging stride across the meadow.

The girl, bending above the water, suddenly struck sharply with her paddle.

Instantly the man halted in his tracks, knee deep in clover.

Maryette, apparently unconscious of his presence, continued to soap and scrub and slap her wash, singing in her clear, untrained voice of a child the chansonette she had made that morning. But out of the corner of her eyes she kept him in view—saw him come sauntering forward as though reassured, became aware that he had approached very near, was standing behind her.

Turning presently, where she knelt, to pick up another soiled garment, she suddenly encountered his dark gaze; and her start and slight exclamation were entirely genuine.

"*Mon Dieu!*" she said, with offended emphasis, "one does not approach people that way, without a word!"

"Did I frighten mademoiselle?" he asked, in recognizable French, but with an accent unpleasantly familiar to her. "If I did, I am very sorry and I offer mademoiselle a thousand excuses and apologies."

The girl, kneeling there in the clover, flashed a smile at him over her shoulder. The quick colour reddened his face and powerful neck. The girl had been right; her smile had been an answer that he was not going to ignore.

"What a pretty spot for a *lavoir*," he said, stepping to the edge of the pool; "and what a pretty girl to adorn it!"

Maryette tossed her head:

"Be pleased to pass your way, monsieur. Do you not perceive that I am busy?"

"It is not impossible to exchange a polite word or two when people are busy, is it, mademoiselle?" he asked, laughing and showing a white and perfect set of teeth under a short, dark mustache.

She continued to wring out her wash; but there was now a slight smile on her lips.

"May I not say who I am?" he asked persuasively. "May I not venture to speak?"

"*Mon dieu*, monsieur, there is liberty of

speech for all in France. That blackbird might be glad to know your name if you choose to tell him."

"But I ask *your* permission to speak to *you!*" There seemed to be no sense of humour in this young man.

She laughed:

"I am not curious to hear who you are! . . . But if it affords you any relief to explain to the west wind what your name may be—" She ended with a disdainful shrug. After a moment she lifted her pretty eyes to his—lovely, provocative, tormenting eyes. But they were studying the stranger closely.

He was a powerfully built, dark-skinned young man in the familiar khaki of the American muleteers, wearing their insignia, their cap, their holster and belt, and an extra pouch or wallet, loaded evidently with something heavy.

She said, coolly:

"You must be one of the new Yankee muleteers who came with that beautiful new herd of mules."

He laughed:

"Yes, I'm an American muleteer. My name is Charles Braun. I came over in the last transport."

"You know Steek?"

"Who?"

"Steek! Monsieur Steekee Smeete?"

"Sticky Smith?"

"*Mais oui?*"

"I've met him," he replied curtly.

"And Monsieur Keed Glenn?"

"I've met Kid Glenn, too. Why?"

"They are friends of mine—very intimate friends. Of course," she added, nose up-tilted, "if they are not also *your* friends, any acquaintance with me will be very difficult for *you*, Monsieur Braun."

He laughed easily and seated himself on the grass beside her; and, as he sat down, a metallic clinking sounded in his wallet.

"*Tenez*," she remarked, "you carry old iron and bottles about with you, I notice."

"Snaffles, curbs and stirrup irons," he replied carelessly. And in the girl's heart there leaped the swift, fierce flame of certainty in suspicion.

"Why do you bring all that ironmongery down here?" she inquired, with frankly childish curiosity, leisurely wringing out her linen.

"A mule got away from the corral. I've been wandering around in the bushes trying to find him," he explained, so naturally and in such a friendly voice that she raised her eyes to look again at this young gallant who lingered here at the *lavoir* for the sake of her *beaux yeux*.

Could this dark-eyed, smiling youth be a Hun spy? His smooth, boyish features, his crisp short hair and tiny mustache shading lips a trifle too red and overfull did not displease her. In his way he was handsome.

His voice, too, was attractive, gaily persuasive, but it was his pronunciation of the letters c and d which had instantly set her on her guard.

Seated on the bank near her, his roving eyes full of bold curiosity bent on her from time to time, his idle fingers plaiting a little wreath out of long-stemmed clover and *boutons d'or*, he appeared merely an intrusive, irresponsible young fellow willing to amuse

328

himself with a few moments' rustic courtship here before he continued on his way.

"You are exceedingly pretty," he said. "Will you tell me your name in exchange for mine?"

"Maryette Courtray."

"Oh," he exclaimed in quick recognition; "you are bell-mistress in Sainte Lesse, then! *You* are the celebrated carillonnette! I have heard about you. I suspected that you might be the little mistress of Sainte Lesse bells, because you wear the Legion—" He nodded his handsome head toward the decoration on her blouse.

"And to think," he added effusively, "that it is just a mere slip of a girl who was decorated for bravery by France!"

She smiled at him with all the beguilingly *bête* innocence of the young when flattered:

"You are too amiable, monsieur. I really do not understand why they gave me the Legion. To encourage all French children, perhaps—because I really am a dreadful coward." She tapped the holster on her thigh and gazed at him quite guilelessly out of wide and trustful eyes. "You see? I dare not even come here to wash my clothes unless I carry this—in case some Boche comes prowling."

"Whose pistol is it?" he asked.

"The weapon belongs to Monsieur Steek. When I come to wash here I borrow it."

"Are you the sweetheart of Monsieur Steek?" he inquired, mimicking her pronunciation of "Stick," and at the same time fixing his dark eyes boldly and expressively on hers.

"Does a young girl of my age have sweethearts?" she demanded scornfully.

"If she hasn't had one, it's time," he returned, staring hard at her with a persistent and fixed smile that had become almost offensive.

"Oh, la!" she exclaimed with a shrug of her youthful shoulders. "Perhaps you think I have time for such foolishness—what with housework to do and washing, and caring for my father, and my duties in the belfry every day!"

"Youth passes swiftly, belle Maryette."

"Imitate him, beau monsieur, and swiftly pass your way!"

"*L'amour est doux, petite Marie!*"

"*Je m'en moque!*"

He rose, smiling confidently, dropped on his knees beside her, and rolled back his cuffs.

"Come," he said, "I'll help you wash. We two should finish quickly."

"I am in no haste."

"But it will give you an hour's leisure, belle Maryette."

"Why should I wish for leisure, beau monsieur?"

"I shall try to instruct you why, when we have our hour together."

"Do you mean to pay court to me?"

"I am doing that now. My ardent courtship will already be accomplished, so that we need not waste our hour together!" He began to laugh and wring out the linen.

"Monsieur," she expostulated smilingly, "your apropos disturbs me. Have you the assurance to believe that you already appeal to my heart?"

"Have I not appealed to it a little, Mary-ette?"

The girl averted her head coquettishly. For a few minutes they scrubbed away there together, side by side on their knees above the rim of the pool. Then, without warning, his hot, red lips burned her neck. Her swift recoil was also a shudder; her face flushed.

"Don't do that!" she said sharply, straightening up in the grass where she was kneeling.

"You are so adorable!" he pleaded in a low, tense voice.

There was a long silence. She had moved aside and away from him on her knees; her head remained turned, too, and her features were set as though carven out of rosy marble.

She was summoning every atom of resolution, every particle of courage to do what she must do. Every fibre in her revolted with the effort; but she steeled herself, and at last the forced smile was stamped on her lips, and she dared turn her head and meet his burning gaze.

"You frighten me," she said—and her unsteady voice was convincing. "A young girl is not courted so abruptly."

"Forgive me," he murmured. "I could not help myself—your neck is so fragrant, so childlike——"

"Then you should treat me as you would a child!" she retorted pettishly. "Amuse me, if you aspire to any comradeship with me. Your behaviour does not amuse me at all."

"We shall become comrades," he said confidently, "and you shall be sufficiently amused."

"It requires time for two people to become comrades."

"Will you give me an hour this evening?"

"What? A rendezvous?" she exclaimed, laughing.

"Yes."

"You mean somewhere alone with you?"

"Will you, Maryette?"

"But why? I am not yet old enough for such foolishness. It would not amuse me at all to be alone with you for an hour." She pouted and shrugged and absently plucked a hollow stem from the sedge.

"It would amuse me much more to sit here

and blow bubbles," she added, clearing the stem with a quick breath and soaping the end of it.

Then, with tormenting malice, she let her eyes rest sideways on him while she plunged the hollow stem into the water, withdrew it, dripping, and deliberately blew an enormous golden bubble from the end.

"Look!" she cried, detaching the bubble, apparently enchanted to see it float upward. "Is it not beautiful, my fairy balloon?"

On her knees there beside the basin she blew bubble after bubble, detaching each with a slight movement of her wrist, and laughing delightedly to see them mount into the sunshine.

"You *are* a child," he said, worrying his red underlip with his teeth. "You're a baby, after all."

She said:

"Very well, then, children require toys to amuse them, not sighs and kisses and bold, brown eyes to frighten and perplex them. Have you any toys to amuse me if I give you an hour with me?"

"Maryette, I can easily teach you——"

"No! Will you bring me a toy to amuse me?—a clay pipe to blow bubbles? I adore bubbles."

"If I promise to amuse you, will you give me an hour?" he asked.

"How can I?" she demanded with sudden caprice. "I have my wash to finish; then I have to see that my father has his soup; then I must attend to customers at the inn, go up to the belfry, oil the machinery, play the carillon later, wind the drum for the night——"

"I shall come to you in the tower after the angelus," he said eagerly.

"I shall be too busy——"

"After the carillon, then! Promise, Maryette!"

"And sit up there alone with you in the dark for an hour? *Ma foi!* How amusing!" She laughed in pretty derision. "I shall not even be able to blow bubbles!"

Watching her pouting face intently, he said:

"Suppose I bring some toy balloons for you

to fly from the clock tower? Would that amuse you—you beautiful, perverse child?"

"Little toy balloons!" she echoed, enchanted. "What pleasure to set them afloat from the belfry! Do you really promise to bring me some little toy balloons to fly?"

"Yes. But *you* must promise not to speak about it to anybody."

"Why?"

"Because the gendarmes wouldn't let us fly any balloons."

"You mean that they might think me a spy?" she inquired naïvely.

"Or me," he rejoined with a light laugh. "So we shall have to be very discreet and go cautiously about our sport. And it ought to be great fun, Maryette, to sail balloons out over the German trenches. We'll tie a message to every one! Shall we, little comrade?"

She clapped her hands.

"That *will* enrage the Boches!" she cried. "You won't forget to bring the balloons?"

"After the carillon," he nodded, staring at her intently.

"Half past ten," she said; "not one minute

earlier. I cannot be disturbed when playing. Do you understand? Do you promise?"

"Yes," he said, "I promise not to bother you before half past ten."

"Very well. Now let me do my washing here in peace."

She was still scrubbing her linen when he went reluctantly away across the meadow toward Sainte Lesse. And when she finally stood up, swung the basket to her head, and left the meadow, the sun hung low behind Sainte Lesse Wood and a rose and violet glow possessed the world.

At the White Doe Inn she flew feverishly about her duties, aiding the ancient peasant woman with the simple preparations for dinner, giving her father his soup and helping him to bed, swallowing a mouthful herself as she hastened to finish her household tasks.

Kid Glenn came in as usual for an *aperitif* while she was gathering up her wooden gloves.

"Did a mule stray today from your corral?" she asked, filling his glass for him.

"No," he said.

"Are you sure?"

"Dead certain. Why?"

"Do you know one of the new muleteers named Braun?"

"I know him by sight."

"Keed!" she said, going up to him and placing both hands on his broad shoulders; "I play the carillon after the angelus. Bring Steek to the bell-tower half an hour after you hear the carillon end. You will hear it end; you will hear the quarter hour strike presently. Half an hour later, after the third quarter hour strikes, you shall arrive. Bring pistols. Do you promise?"

"Sure! What's the row, Maryette?"

"I don't know yet. I *think* we shall find a spy in the tower."

"Where?"

"In the belfry, *parbleu!* And you and Steek shall come up the stairs and you shall wait in the dark, there where the keyboard is, and where you see all the wires leading upward. You shall listen attentively, and I will be on the landing above, among my

338

bells. And when you hear me cry out to you, then you shall come running with pistols!"

"For heaven's sake——"

"Is it understood? Give me your word, Keed!"

"Sure!——"

"*Allons! Assez!*" she whispered excitedly. "Make prisoner any man you see there!— *any* man! You understand?"

"You bet!"

"*Any man!*" she repeated slowly, "even if he wears the same uniform *you* wear."

There was a silence. Then:

"By God!" said Glenn under his breath.

"You suspect?"

"Yes. And if it *is* one of our German-American muleteers, we'll lynch him!" he whispered in a white rage.

But Maryette shook her head.

"No," she said in a dull, even voice, "let the gendarmerie take him in charge. Spy or suspect, he must have his chance. That is the law in France."

"You don't give rats a chance, do you?"

339

"I give everything its chance," she said simply. "And so does my country."

She drew the automatic pistol from her holster, examined it, raised her eyes gravely to the American beside her:

"This is terrible for me," she added, in a low but steady voice. "If it were not for my country—" She made a grave gesture, turned, and went slowly out through the arched stone passage into the main street of the town. A few minutes later the angelus sounded sweetly over the woods and meadows of Sainte Lesse.

At ten, as the last stroke of the hour ended, there came a charming, intimate little murmur of awakening bells; it grew sweeter, clearer, filling the starry sky, growing, exquisitely increasing in limpid, transparent volume, sweeping through the high, dim belfry like a great wind from Paradise carrying Heaven's own music out over the darkened earth.

All Sainte Lesse came to its doorways to listen to the playing of their beloved Carillonnette; the bell-music ebbed and swelled under the stars; the ancient Flemish masterpiece, written by some carillonneur whose bones had long been dust, became magnificently vital again under the enchanted hands of the little mistress of the bells.

In fifteen minutes the carillon ended; a slight pause followed, then the quarter hour struck.

With the last stroke of the bell, the girl drew off her wooden gloves, laid them on the keyboard, turned slowly in her seat, listening. A slight sound coming from the spiral staircase of stone set her heart beating violently. Had the suspected man violated his word? She drew the automatic pistol from her holster, rose, and stole up to the stone platform overhead, where, rising tier on tier into the darkness, the great carillon of Sainte Lesse loomed overhead.

She listened uneasily. Had the man lied? It seemed to her as though her hammering heart must burst from her bosom with the terrible suspense of the moment.

Suddenly a shadowy form appeared at the

head of the stairs, reaching the platform at one bound. And her heart seemed to stop as she realized that this man had arrived too early for her friends to be of any use to her. He had lied to her. And now she must take him unaided, or kill him there in the starlight under the looming bells.

"Maryette!" he called. She did not stir.

"Maryette!" he whispered. "Where are you, little sweetheart? Forgive me, I could not wait any longer. I adore you——"

All at once he discovered her standing motionless in the shadow of the great bell Bayard—sprang toward her, eager, ardent, triumphant.

"Maryette," he whispered, "I love you! I shall teach you what a lover is——"

Suddenly he caught a glimpse of her face; the terrible expression in her eyes checked him.

"What has happened?" he asked, bewildered. And then he caught sight of the pistol in her hand.

"What's that for?" he demanded harshly. "Are you afraid to love me? Do you think

I'm the kind of lover to stop for a thing like that——"

She said, in a low, distinct voice:

"Don't move! Put up both hands instantly!"

"What!" he snapped out, like the crack of a lash.

"I know who you are. You're a Boche and no Yankee! Turn your back and raise your arms!"

For a moment they looked at each other.

"I think," she said, steadily, "you had better explain your gas cylinders and balloons to the gendarmes at the Poste."

"No," he said, "I'll explain them to you, *now!*——"

"If you touch your pistol, I fire!——"

But already he had whipped out his pistol; and she fired instantly, smashing his right hand to pulp.

"You damned hell-cat!" he screamed, stretching out his shattered hand in an agony of impotent fury. Blood rained from it on the stone flags. Suddenly he started toward her.

"Don't stir!" she whispered. "Turn your back and raise both arms!"

His face became ghastly.

"Let me go, in God's name!" he burst out in a strangled voice. "Don't send me before a firing squad! Listen to me, little comrade —I surrender myself to your mercy——"

"Then keep away from me! Keep your distance!" she cried, retreating. He followed, fawning:

"Listen! We were such good comrades——"

"Don't come any nearer to me!" she called out sharply; but he still shuffled toward her, whimpering, drenched in blood, both hands uplifted.

"Kamerad!" he whined, "Kamerad—" and suddenly launched a kick at her.

She just avoided it, springing behind the bell Bayard; and he rushed at her and struck with both uplifted arms, showering her with blood, but not quite reaching her.

In the darkness among the beams and the deep shadows of the bells she could hear him hunting for her, breathing heavily and making ferocious, inarticulate noises, as she swung herself up onto the first beam above and continued to crawl upward.

"Where are you, little fool?" he cried at length. "I have business with you before I cut your throat—that smooth, white throat of yours that I kissed down there by the *lavoir!*" There was no sound from her.

He went back toward the stairs and began hunting about in the starlight for his pistol; but there was no parapet on the bell platform, and he probably concluded that it had fallen over the edge of the tower into the street.

Supporting his wounded hand, he stood glaring blankly about him, and his bloodshot eyes presently fell on the door to the stairs. But he must have realized that flight would be useless for him if he left this girl alive in her bell-tower, ready to alarm the town the moment he ran for the stairs.

With his left hand he fumbled under his tunic and disengaged a heavy trench knife from its sheath. The loss of blood was making his legs a trifle unsteady, but he pulled himself together and moved stealthily under

the shadows of beam and bell until he came
to the spot he selected. And there he lay
down, the hilt of the knife in his left hand,
the blade concealed by his opened tunic.

His heavy groans at last had their effect
on the girl, who had climbed high up into the
darkness, creeping from beam to beam and
mounting from one tier of bells to another.

Standing on the lowest beam, she cautiously
looked out through an oubliette and saw him
lying on his back near the sheer edge of the
roof.

Evidently he, also, could see her head silhouetted against the stars, for he called up
to her in a plaintive voice that he was bleed-
ing to death and unable to move.

After a few moments, opening his eyes
again, he saw her standing on the roof beside
him, looking down at him. And he whispered
his appeal in the name of Christ. And in
His name the little bell-mistress responded.

When she had used the blue kerchief at her
neck for a tourniquet and had checked the
hemorrhage, he was still patiently awaiting a

better opportunity to employ his knife. It would not do to bungle the affair. And he thought he knew how it could be properly done—if he could get her head in the crook of his muscular elbow.

"Lift me, dear ministering angel," he whispered weakly.

She stooped impulsively, hesitated, then, suddenly terrified at the blazing ferocity in his eyes, she shrank back at the same instant that his broad knife flashed in her very face.

He was on his feet at a bound, and, as she raised her voice in a startled cry for help, he plunged heavily at her, but slipped and fell in his own blood. Then the clattering jingle of spurred boots on the stone stairs below caught his ear. He was trapped, and he realized it. He slowly got to his feet.

As Smith and Glenn appeared, springing out of the low-arched door, the muleteer Braun turned and faced them.

There was a silence, then Glenn said, bitterly:

"It's you, is it, you dirty Dutchman!"

"Hands up!" said Smith quietly. "Come

on, now; it's a case of 'Kamerad' for yours."

Braun did not move to comply with the demand. Gradually it dawned on them that the man was game.

"Maryette!" he called; "where are you?"

Smith said curiously:

"What do you want with her, Braun?"

"I want to speak to her."

"Come over here, Maryette," said Glenn sullenly.

The girl crept out of the shadows. Her face was ghastly.

Braun looked at her with pallid scorn:

"You little, ignorant fool," he said, "I'd have made you a better lover than you'll ever have now!"

He shrugged his square shoulders in contempt, turned without a glance at Smith and Glenn, and stepped outward into space. And as he fell there between sky and earth, hurtling downward under the stars, Glenn's pistol flashed twice, killing his quarry in midair while falling.

"Can you beat it?" he demanded hoarsely, turning on Smith. "Ain't that me all over!

—soft-hearted enough to do that skunk a kindness thataway!"

But his youthful voice was shaking, and he stared at the edge of the abyss, listening to the far tumult now arising from the street below.

"Did you shoot?" he inquired, controlling his nervous voice with an effort.

"Naw," said Smith disgustedly. ". . . Now, Maryette, put one arm around my neck, and me and the Kid will take you down them stairs, because you look tired—kind o' peeked and fussed, what with all this funny business going on——"

"Oh, Steek! Steek!" she sobbed. "Oh, *mon ami*, Steek!"

She began to cry bitterly. Smith picked her up in his arms.

"What you need is sleep," he said very gently.

But she shook her head: she had business to transact on her knees that night—business with the Mother of God that would take all night long—and many, many other sleepless nights; and many candles.

She put her left arm around Smith's neck and hid her tear-wet face on his shoulder. And, as he bore her out of the high tower and descended the unlighted, interminable stairs of stone, he heard her weeping against his breast and softly asking intercession in behalf of a dead young man who had tried to be to her a "Kamerad"—as he understood it—including the entire gamut, from amorous beast to fiend.

There was a single candle lighted in the bar of the White Doe. On the "zinc," side by side, like birds on a rail, sat the two muleteers. In each big, sunburnt fist was an empty glass; their spurred feet dangled; they leaned forward where they sat, hunched up over their knees, heads slightly turned, as though intently listening. A haze of cigarette smoke dimmed the candle flame.

The drone of an aëroplane high in the midnight sky came to them at intervals. At last the sound died away under the far stars.

By the smoky candle flame Kid Glenn unfolded and once more read the letter that kept them there:

—I ought to get to Sainte Lesse somewhere around midnight. Don't say a word to Maryette.

JACK.

Sticky Smith, reading over his shoulder, slowly rolled another cigarette.

"When Jack comes," he drawled, "it's a-goin' to he'p a lot. That Maryette girl's plumb done in."

"Sure she's done in," nodded Kid Glenn. "Wouldn't it do in anybody to shoot up a young man an' then see him step off the top of a skyscraper?"

Smith admitted that he himself had felt "kind er squeamish." He added: "Gawd, how he spread when he hit them flags! You didn't look at him, did you, Kid?"

"Naw. Say, d'ya think Maryette has gone to bed?"

"I dunno. When we left her up there in her room, I turned and took a peek to see she was comfy, but she was down onto both knees before that china virgin on the niche over her bed."

"She oughter be in bed. You gotta sleep off a thing like that, or you feel punk next day," remarked Glenn, meditatively twirling the last drops of eau-de-vie around in his tumbler. Then he swallowed them and smacked his lips. "She'll come around all O. K. when she sees Jack," he added.

"Goin' to let him wake her up?"

"Can you see us stoppin' him? He'd kick the pants off us——"

"Sh-h-h!" motioned Smith; "there's a automobile! By gum! It's stopped!——"

The two muleteers set their glasses on the bar, slid to the floor, and marched, clanking, into the covered way that led to the street. Smith undid the bolts. A young man stood outside in the starlight.

"Well, Jack Burley, you old son of a gun!" drawled Glenn. "Gawd! You look fit for a dead one!"

"We ain't told her!" whispered Smith. "She an' us done in a Fritz this evening, an' it sorter turned Maryette's stomach——"

"Not that she ain't well," explained Glenn hastily; "only a girl feels different. Stick

352

an' me, we just took a few drinks, but Mary-ette, soon as she got home, she just flopped down on her knees and asked that china vir-gin of hers to go easy on that there Fritz——"

They had conducted Burley to the bar; both their arms were draped around his shoulders; both talked to him at the same time.

"This here Fritz," began Glenn—but Burley freed himself from their embrace.

"Where's Maryette?" he demanded.

Smith jerked a silent thumb toward the ceiling.

"In bed?"

"Or prayin'."

Burley flushed, hesitated.

"G'wan up, anyway," said Glenn. "I reckon it'll do her a heap o' good to lamp you, you old son of a gun!"

Burley turned, went up the short flight of stairs to her closed door. There was candle-light shining through the transom. He knocked with a trembling hand. There was no answer. He knocked again; heard her uncertain step; stepped back as her door opened.

The girl, a drooping figure in her night robe, stood listlessly on the threshold. Which of the muleteers it was who had come to her door she did not notice. She said:

"I am very tired. Death is a dreadful thing. I can't put it from my mind. I am trying to pray——"

She lifted her weary eyes and found herself looking into the face of her own lover. She turned very white, lovely eyes dilated.

"Is—is it thou, Djack?"

"C'est moi, ma ploo belle!"

She melted into his tightening arms with a faint cry. Very high overhead, under the lustrous stars, an aëroplane droned its uncharted way across a blood-soaked world.

(1)